Christmas Wishes and Holiday Kisses

Written By: Kelly McDonough

PublishAmerica
Baltimore

ISBN: 1-4241-4684-4
PUBLISHED BY PUBLISHAMERICA, LLLP
www.publishamerica.com
Baltimore

Printed in the United States of America

MAKE-BELIEVE BRIDE by Kelly McDonough is one book that you simply HAVE to read! Following an unusual storyline, it is intriguing and manages to catch the reader's interest from the very first page and sustain it throughout. The background of the story is impeccable. The comebacks between Kelsey and Jonathan are refreshing, and the style is sharp, all in all, this is one book I would not advise on missing out!"
— **Jennifer Ashraf, Rising Star Magazine, Bangladesh**

"The author has given such details that the reader will feel the sand beneath their feet, they'll feel the breeze blowing off the ocean, and see the stars shining overhead. This is definitely a book for the keeper shelf."
— **Five angel review.** — Donna, Fallen Angels

"This is a very interesting story, well-written, and keeps you reading just so you know how it ends."
— ***Reviewer's Choice*** — Wilma Frana, Word Museum

"Make-Believe Bride was a pleasure to read. The first thing I did after finishing the final page was sigh in pleasure. I absolutely adored this book. I will look for more titles by Ms. McDonough."
— **Four coffee cups.** — Sue F. Coffetime Romance

"For a relatively short book, Ms. McDonough manages to make each word, each scene and every interaction count and provides a gratifying tale of romance with no filler or fluff. This reviewer recommends Make-Believe Bride to any reader who enjoys contemporary romances with hints of humor, and would enjoy reading further tales about the Trent family in the future."
— **Four and a half hearts.** —Leah, Love Romances

To everyone I love and to those who love me back. Also a special thanks to Patti Chapman for her special "inspiration."

CHAPTER ONE

Eliza shivered. Easy adjusting to earth's climate? Never. Her sleeveless white chiffon dress billowed around her slender ankles and shapely calves as the winter wind chilled her to the bone. She stood on tip-toe to peer once again in the small bedroom window. She smiled. The beautiful child beamed beneath the moonlight.

Just as Eliza made her way over to the livingroom window, she slipped and almost fell. "Well it's a good thing I have on these darn ballet slippers, or surely I would kill myself," she said never considering she should be wearing boots in the snow. Not that she understood about snow. She just sometimes forgot between jobs. She regained her footing and made her way to the large picture window. What she saw caused her to wonder, but that was nothing new. Eliza always wondered about everything. At least that's what Glory, her supervisor, said.

Eliza could only see the profile of the man seated in the recliner. It stood straight, and the man sat staring at the enormous Christmas tree as if in a trance. The colored lights twinkled on and off at different intervals illuminating every kind of angel ornament imaginable. Eliza thought she'd never seen such a grand tree.

So, this was to be her new assignment. She always liked to *case the joint* before diving right into any one job. This one, she thought she could handle, so she'd tell Glory she'd do it.

She held the folded newspaper in her hand and read the advertisement for the tenth time.

Live-in care giver needed for terminally ill elderly woman and six-year-old child. Light housework and cooking required. Room and board included. Good pay and excellent benefits for the right person. Call 570-3637 to set up an interview. References required.

Well she certainly knew how to give care to those in need. As for the housework and cooking—even an angel could learn how to do that, right? She pulled her cell phone from her pocket and dialed the familiar number.

"Glory, I'll take it. Just tell me when and how to start."

"Now Eliza, remember the most important part of this assignment, you are not, I repeat, you are not under any circumstances allowed to become romantically involved with Jason."

"No problem there Glory. I'm not in the market for a human male. What should I wear to the interview?"

"Something soft and feminine, and remember to go over your resume. By tomorrow this time you should be starting your new assignment."

"Gotcha. Over and out," Eliza flipped off the cell phone. Handy little things though there were other ways of communicating on the other side. Glory just thought it a good idea to get her used to modern technology since most of her jobs involved earth. For goodness sakes, she had her on a computer from day one on the job. Eliza would be the first to admit to being a computer klutz. It took a lot of hard work learning how to master the computer. She flew through angel school with high marks until she had to face the computer. Glory promised her that once she *got it*, she'd have it forever. Eliza could proudly say she could now take a computer apart and put it back together in one hour, if not less.

Eliza went back to the angel's side of heaven for one more night. Tomorrow night, hopefully, she'd be moving into her new temporary home.

"I've cared for several terminally ill patients over the years and have worked in a daycare for a short while."

Jason liked the sound of this woman's voice. "You do have references?"

"Of course, from the families I've cared for over the years—and the day care," she added.

"If you could stop by about one o'clock, I'd be happy to see you," Jason said.

"You didn't tell me your address Mr...."

"It's Jason. Jason Abbott, and I live at 36 Cherry lane."

"I'm familiar with the area. I'll look forward to meeting you, Mr. Abbott."

When Eliza hung up, she wondered what would convince Jason Abbott he needed to hire her on the spot. Oh well, the *Big Guy Upstairs* must have some sort of plan. She'd simply have to trust Glory and go to the interview.

Eliza smoothed the soft pastel pink skirt she was wearing. It was very delicate and her blouse equally so. She just loved the hand appliquéd roses on the collar of her white blouse. She picked up her resume and once again went over all the families she worked for in the last several years. Jason could call any one of them and they'd verify Eliza's existence—the reason why angels always kept their names the same.

Eliza pulled up the collar of her long pink coat and stepped onto the old Victorian's wrap-around porch. She noted the extensive detail and how the house seemed to be well cared for. Before she could even knock, Jason answered the door.

Eliza stood stock still standing face-to-face with one of the most gorgeous human males on the planet. No wonder Glory made her promise not to get romantically involved.

Jason snapped her out of her reverie by extending his hand. "I'm Jason Abbott, and this here is Angel Abbott," he said his one hand resting on the shoulder of a child wrapped around his leg. It was the same little girl Eliza had peeked in on the previous night. Eliza couldn't help thinking how she lived up to her name because the little girl had precious angel qualities.

"I hope you don't mind if Angel sits in on the interview."

"Well, I think that's a fine idea since she's the one who's going to be boss."

Angel giggled. Her father on the other hand was quick to correct, "The child who needs tending and lots of care."

Eliza held out her hand to Angel. "It's nice meeting you, Angel. Did anyone ever tell you, you look like one?"

Angel looked up at her Dad and smiled. "My Dad does all the time, and my Mom used to. I don't remember her much because I was only three-years-old when she died, but Daddy tells me all about her and me, and he said the minute she first saw me I looked like an angel. That's why my name is Angel."

Jason's smile faded and there was a faraway look in his eyes. He quickly recovered. "Please, come in out of the cold. We're having one of the worst winters ever. I think we've had at least a week of record setting low temperatures."

"I'm not much of a winter person, but I do like sleigh riding and making angels in the snow when it's not too cold."

Angel smiled at Eliza. Bingo, she'd hit her mark.

"Make yourself comfortable," Jason said gesturing to the couch. He and Angel sat across from her on the love seat. "This really is an informal interview. I'm looking for someone who can care for my Mom. She's seventy-eight and dying of cancer. She's going through chemo' treatments right now, but it doesn't look good. We do have some help from hospice. Anyway," Jason sighed, "that part of the job will probably be temporary, but I'll still need to keep someone on to look after Angel. I guess you could say, I'll be needing a nanny. My Mom used to take care of Angel before she got sick."

Eliza looked at Jason and she could feel his pain. A gift given to her by the *Big Man Upstairs*. God gave angels all kinds of gifts. Eliza had the gift of feeling another's feelings. Sometimes she wished it wasn't

10

so because she hurt when people hurt, and right now she felt the tears in his eyes that weren't visible. This poor man, who couldn't be more than thirty-eight, had lost his wife and his mother seemed next in line for the other side. "How is your father taking all of this?" Eliza gently asked.

"My Dad passed away many years ago. I'm surprised Mom lived this long. She always said she couldn't live without him. He'd had a history of heart problems. My wife—well let's just say cancer has made its rounds in this house."

Impulsively, Eliza got up and sat next to Jason and Angel. She grabbed Jason's hand. "You poor, poor man. What you must have gone through—are going through. Whether I get this job or not, I'd be more than willing to help you."

That cinched it for Jason. Something about this woman made him feel he could trust her... All he needed was Angel's approval, and he'd hire Eliza on the spot.

"Thank you," Jason said, truly touched by this stranger's empathy, "If you could give me a few moments alone with Angel, I'd appreciate it."

"Take your time, Jason."

Once in the kitchen, Jason asked, "So what do you think, Angel? Would she make a good nanny?"

"I like her Daddy."

"Then, I'll hire her if that's all right with you. I mean, honey, you're the one who's going to be spending a lot of time with her. Do you have any questions for her?"

Angel nodded, "Just one."

"Then, let's go ask her."

Jason and Angel walked back to the drawing room. Jason's larger hand swallowed up Angel's smaller one. They sat back on the love seat where Eliza still sat.

"Miss Eliza," Angel addressed the angel sitting next to her, "How do you feel about taking care of a puppy, too?"

Eliza smiled at Angel. She loved animals. "Do you have one?" she asked.

11

Angel shook her head. "Not yet anyway," the little girl with the beautiful blonde curls looked up at her Dad. Jason just shook his head, smiled and said to his daughter, "You got me."

"It's not a problem for me to care for a puppy, too," Eliza said cautiously. She got the distinct feeling this had been an issue between Angel and her father.

"You're hired. When can you move in?"

It surprised Eliza how quickly Jason had come to a decision. There was no talk about her past work, no serious questions… The *Big Guy Upstairs* sure did have a plan, and now she wondered what she'd gotten herself into.

"I'm ready to stay the night. I just have to grab some clothes and toiletries. Then, tomorrow I can move my belongings in. I don't have much."

"I'm sorry Eliza, I didn't even tell you what the job pays. It's five hundred dollars a week with complete benefits and room and board. Is that satisfactory?" Jason didn't breathe for a minute hoping she'd accept his offer. He wasn't a poor man by any means. He was a contractor who made lots of money, but the treatments and medical expenses for both his wife and mother had drained his savings account over the years.

"I'd say that's more than a fair offer," Eliza reached for Jason's hand again, "What's your Mom's name?"

"Vera. Vera Abbott."

Eliza could feel Jason's pain as he said his mother's name. He had a hard time expressing his emotions. She could feel it. The feelings surrounded him.

"And how is Angel handling all this?" Eliza asked despite the fact the little girl remained in the room.

"Good question. Honey?" Jason turned to his daughter.

"My grandma is real sick, and she's going to heaven real soon to be with my grandpa and Mommy."

It surprised Eliza how simply the little girl put it. Eliza didn't feel any pain coming from Angel, just a simple awareness of everything going on all around her. Interesting.

"Let me show you your room. Then you can bring in some of your things you need for the night. Once you're moved in tomorrow, I'll introduce you to my mother."

Jason led Eliza up a wide staircase furnished with a beautiful cherry wood banister. It curved up to what looked to be like three floors, but they got off on the second. Quickly, Jason ushered Eliza into a spacious room with a large canopy bed.

"I hope you find this room acceptable. We can paint or change anything in it you don't like or that would make you feel more comfortable."

"My harp."

"Excuse me?" Jason looked at Eliza.

"I'll only need add my harp to make this room just perfect," she turned to Jason, and in doing so, her long blonde hair swung around her shoulders, "I love the old woodwork and the flowered wallpaper and the hardwood floors are exquisite as are the oriental rugs."

Jason sighed his relief. "My mother's room is directly across from this one, so I hoped you'd like it. Angel's room is down the hall, but a lot of the times she sleeps with me. I'm on the first floor. She sometimes has bad dreams... I'm hoping with you here, she'll adjust better to being on her own."

Well that explained why she saw Angel sleeping with her father last night. She wondered why Jason slept on the first floor in a small room when there seemed to *be an abundance of bedrooms on this floor.*

As if to answer her question, Jason said, "My wife and I slept up here in the master bedroom, but once she died I couldn't bring myself to sleeping in that room. We had plans to fill up all these bedrooms with little ones, but it looks like God had a different plan.

God. The one thing she didn't really think about until now. How did Jason feel about God after all he'd been through? She decided to broach the subject.

"Sometimes it seems like God isn't listening to our prayers."

"After Kathleen's death, I thought I'd never step foot in a church again. My Mom changed that. She insisted I not give up on Him. To be honest with you, Eliza, I don't really know what I feel about God these days, but I teach Angel her prayers and to have faith. It's the only thing that'll pull you through, I guess."

"I guess," Eliza carefully continued with her next statement, "My parents died in a car accident and I don't have any brothers or sisters. You can say I'm alone—no children to look after," she reached out and touched Angel's cheek, "until now, or should I say, once again?" Eliza had spoken the truth. Glory had told her all about the accident that claimed her parents and her own life. She simply went on to become an angel. Her parents settled in the other side of heaven.

"Do you need any help getting your things?" Jason asked Eliza sensing her mind wasn't all there.

"Oh, no. I'll be on my way and back in about an hour or two, if that's all right with you?"

"That'll be fine. We'll have supper waiting for you. Just don't expect anything beyond hamburgers and hotdogs from me," Jason laughed. The sound made her feel… well, it instantly made Eliza happy, and for the second time that day, she realized just how attractive her new assignment could be.

CHAPTER TWO

Glory met Eliza in the park as planned. Eliza looked at her mentor. What a beautiful woman now looked at her. She had long dark hair and the longest eyelashes she'd ever seen, but her chocolate brown eyes instantly made Eliza trust her. Her eyes spoke of sympathy and understanding. Glory knew how badly Eliza missed her parents even though she did good on earth.

"So, my friend, what do you think of your new assignment?"

"I think Jason Abbott and his daughter are hurting, but each show it in different ways."

"Did you find him attractive?"

Eliza decided not to lie to her mentor. "I think he's the most beautiful human male I have ever encountered."

"And do you find his personality pleasing?"

"It's hard to tell so soon, but if my feelings serve me correctly, then yes, yes, I do find him quite the package, and the beautiful little girl is only an added bonus. Some woman is going to be very lucky to win them over."

"Yes, well that's what we're here to talk about. You're job is not only to help with the bridging between life and death, it's to help Jason Abbott move on and find another wife and mother for his daughter. So you've got your hands full."

Eliza sighed. "It won't be hard finding a woman who wants them, but I have a feeling, and we know the *Big Guy Upstairs* gave me good feelings, he's not in the least bit interested in any woman that isn't Kathleen."

"Which is what makes this a challenge. I have a message for you from The Chief. If you successfully complete this assignment, you can be reunited with your parents."

Eliza's eyes lit up as bright as the Christmas tree she'd only seen the previous night. "You mean, I'll be able to see them again? Really?"

"Really. Now, remember, Jason is off limits. You're not his wife and Angel's mother. You're his caretaker and healer and angel to watch over them so that everything turns out just right."

"I understand. Glory, I've got to go to them now."

"I wish you well, my friend," and Glory disappeared as quickly as she'd come.

Eliza sat on the park bench for a long while after Glory disappeared trying to absorb the importance of this new mission and what it personally meant to her. With this assignment, the stakes were high.

This time, Eliza really took in the structure of the house as she approached it from her car which she parked out front, not in the driveway. A beautiful reminder of days gone by. Every nook, every cranny, every windowsill, every turret, every decorative piece was well taken care of to the point of perfection. Even the roof with icicles hanging down looked to be new, and she loved the corner room on the second floor that looked like a castle. She figured it must be the master bedroom from what she'd seen of the inside so far. It was evident Jason took exceptional care of this house. She even loved the color of the house, a muted shade of pink.

This time, Eliza did get a chance to knock. She took a deep breath and hung on to her overnight bag. Jason answered with no Angel in sight. He smiled. Such a simple thing, and it made Eliza's heart flutter. It would make any normal female's heart feel that way she told herself.

16

"We just started eating. I hope you like Chinese. We decided to order out tonight."

"It so happens, I love Chinese, and tomorrow night you'll have a home cooked meal. I'll make sure of it."

"Thanks. It'll be good to have some old-fashioned home cooking again."

Eliza crossed her fingers that she'd do a good job. Jason took her bag. "I'll take this up to your room. You can go into the kitchen and join Angel. She couldn't wait to eat, so I told her to dive right into the food."

Eliza did as instructed. The minute Angel saw Eliza, she lit up. "Miss Eliza, you're here."

"It's okay if you just call me Eliza. As a matter of fact, I prefer it."

"Okay, if you say so."

"Speaking of names, I'd rather you refer to me as Jason not Mr. Abbott. That makes me feel so old," Jason laughed as he crossed to his chair at the table.

"You're not old, Daddy," Angel giggled.

"Well, Angel Girl, some days I'm older than others."

"But, you're not going to get sick are you, Daddy?" Angel had a panic stricken look on her face.

Eliza instantly felt Angel's fear. She knew it terrified Angel to think that something could happen to her father. She decided to let Jason handle the situation. She'd watch how the two interacted and would learn.

"Sweetheart, I'm as healthy as a horse. No need to get worried about me being sick."

"Promise?" Angel asked in a scared little girl's voice.

Jason reached out and ruffled his daughter's hair, "Promise and pinky swear," he held out his pinky, and Angel smiled as they linked fingers.

Eliza caught the strong bond between father and daughter. Jason Abbott? How to define him? Definitely a good man, she didn't question that, and Angel just ached for a mama. Well, she would do her very best to ease Angel's worries and nightmares.

After dinner finished, Eliza immediately began clearing the table. Jason got up to join her.

"Oh no, Jason, you're not to do the housekeeping that's my job now," she said sincerely.

In an equally sincere tone Jason said, "Eliza, I like helping out with some things. I hope you're going to be all right with that. It's just my way, but the cooking… I leave to you."

Oh great Eliza thought *the one thing I can't do.*

Eliza tossed the paper plates and food containers into the trash can where Jason immediately took out the bag and tied it up. "So you play the harp? That's not exactly a common thing," he said as he hefted the bag over his shoulder.

Eliza laughed because she knew it to be the most common thing among the angels, but Jason Abbott had no way of knowing that. "Yes, well, I fell in love with the sound and had to learn myself how to play."

"You're self-taught?" Jason seemed surprised.

"Let's just say it's an intuitive thing."

"You'll have to give me and Angel the pleasure of hearing you play some day."

Again Eliza laughed. "Oh, don't worry. You'll hear me practicing. You'll probably come knocking on my door demanding I put a stop to it."

Jason looked, really looked, at Eliza. He couldn't deny her beauty. Her hair reminded him of his daughter's, blonde and wavy, and she had the most expressive blue eyes. Even her figure seemed perfect. If she hadn't been so compassionate, he might have thought her to be a bit above everyone else—a model type, but he knew differently. She might look like a model, but she had a good heart. He knew it from their conversation on the phone. Her interview only confirmed his feelings. He wondered why she never married. Maybe she had a boyfriend. He'd have to let her know she should feel free to invite him to dinner and for visits.

"Well, what's the routine around here?" Eliza asked wondering what to do next.

"I usually go to my office while Angel plays with her dolls or toys. Then, I usually give her a bath, get her ready for bed and read her a bedtime story. She has to get up at seven a.m. to be ready for school."

"And which of those tasks will I be assuming?"

"Maybe you could play with Angel while I work, and I'm sure she won't mind you giving her a bath, but I'd like to read her to sleep. It's one thing we've always done since my wife passed on."

"Certainly," Eliza felt an overwhelming sense of unhappiness. The healing for Jason had just begun, and Angel? She had her theories about those nightmares. She held out her hand, "Angel, why don't you take me to your playroom, and we'll figure out something to do."

"Oh, I don't have a playroom. I just keep all my toys in the living room. You'll like it in there. We have a really big Christmas tree."

Satisfied that his daughter seemed content, Jason headed to the garbage can outside and then to his office. He could hear Angel giggling as she and Eliza walked through the rooms. He wondered what Eliza said to make that happen. Angel didn't laugh often, but in the few hours since she'd met Eliza, she'd giggled and smiled more than she had in three years.

Eliza stood in awe of the twelve-foot Christmas tree. It seemed to be as wide, too. She delicately handled some of the angel ornaments. One looked like a little girl angel holding a bunny. Another could have doubled for cupid. "These are incredible," Eliza said not realizing she spoke out loud.

"My Mom picked each and every one of these out for me. Daddy says one day when I grow up, I can take them for my family."

"Yes, well that's quite a ways off, Pumpkin," Eliza touched her finger to Angel's nose, "So let's let you be a kid. What shall it be? Dolls or Barbies?"

Angel wrinkled her nose. "Aren't Barbies dolls?"

"A good question. I meant baby dolls you diaper and dress and feed and take for walks in the stroller."

"Oh," Angel thought for a moment, "I don't have any of that kind, but I can ask Santa to bring me some. Would you like that?"

KELLY MCDONOUGH

"Honey, you're so sweet. It's what you like that matters."

"Well, in that case, I'm going to put it down on my list, but we can play Barbies for now."

"Show me your dolls," Eliza said looking at the tree once again. She felt a sudden surge of all the love Angel's mother put into the tree. Every angel was hand picked with love.

"Come here," Angel held out her hand, and Eliza grabbed on, "These are my Barbies and this is their house."

Eliza knelt down on the floor. Unlike the other rooms in the house, this deep rose-colored plush rug covered the floor wall-to-wall. The world of dolls and dreams caught up with Eliza before she knew it.

"This is Alex. He's going to marry Barbie because he has a little girl that needs a mama." Angel held the two dolls together.

"And what's the little girl's name?" Eliza asked.

"Kelly. Barbie has a sister named Kelly too, but this is a different Kelly."

Two hours and many Barbie scenes later, Eliza suggested Angel have her bath.

"Okay, I'll show you where everything is," Angel escorted Eliza to her room on the second floor. From there, Eliza managed to find a nightgown and underwear and robe and slippers.

"You can't forget these," Angel said in an almost reverent voice, "This brush and comb is the one my Mommy always used on me. It's special. See?" Angel held the silver brush up for Eliza to read.

The inscription simply said, *For my angel baby.*

"We won't forget them," Eliza assured Angel, "Do you have any baby powder or lotions you put on after your bath?"

"They're downstairs in the bathroom."

"Then, let's go," Eliza let Angel lead the way. The size of the bathroom surprised her. It looked to be the size of two rooms. The Jacuzzi sat in the one corner, an extra large bathtub off to the side, an entire wall of mirrors and vanity top and the color seemed to be a most delicate shade of pink. Everything else seemed to be white with pink rosebuds: the shower curtain, the toilet seat cover, the carpets,

20

the garbage can, the tissue box holder. Everything matched perfectly. It looked like something right out of a Victorian magazine. The white wicker furniture offset the room nicely.

Eliza started to run the bath, testing the water with her hand while Angel lined up the baby powder and her brush and comb on the vanity top. Once the water filled high enough, Eliza helped Angel undress and settle in the tub.

"This is the soap I always use," Angel pronounced as she proceeded to squirt pink soap from a can.

"Well, that's a first for me. I've never seen foam soap in a can before. What if you turn pink?" Eliza teased.

Angel giggled. "I even have little pills you drop into the water to make it change colors. Only we're all out of them. Daddy said he has to get some more at the store."

"Yes, well, let's scrub up, and do you have a nail brush?"

Angel nodded as she handed over the brush to Eliza. Twenty minutes later, a clean and fresh Angel stood dressed in a white nightgown with a bunny on it and smelled like heaven. She clung to a big pink bear. Pink seemed to be the popular color at the Abbott's house. Eliza realized that must have been the reason why Glory suggested she wear her pink skirt set for the interview. Eliza gently brushed the little girl's blonde curls with the silver brush Angel's mother had bought for her daughter.

"I like you," Angel said. It came out of nowhere.

"Well that's good because I'll tell you a secret," she motioned Angel to come closer, "I like you, too," she whispered.

"Daddy likes you. I can tell."

"Well I'm glad to hear my boss likes me so far. Wait till I play my harp for you. I'll have the two of you eating out of my hand," Eliza smiled a gentle smile.

Angel didn't miss a beat. "Will you teach me how to play?"

"Sure, if it's okay with your Dad."

"If what's okay with your Dad?" Jason had poked his nose in the bathroom.

"Me playing Eliza's harp."

21

"Well, I don't see how that can hurt any. Do you play any other instruments?" Jason wondered aloud.

"No. Just the harp."

"Well, I'm glad to see my best girl is all sparkling clean again," he held out his arms, and Angel ran into them.

"Oh, Daddy, like I'm ever dirty," Angel rolled her eyes.

Jason winked at Eliza, "I know. I'm hoping, come spring, Eliza will show you how to make mud pies."

"Because you haven't lived unless you've made a mud pie," Eliza injected, "I had a nun once tell me that when I was just a girl. I've been making mud pies ever since."

"Well, I'll take over from here," Jason directed to Eliza, "Come on Angel, we'll finish *Sleeping Beauty* tonight."

"Is she sleeping in your room tonight?" Eliza asked.

"Yes, I think we'll have to gradually move her back into her room."

Eliza smiled. "I agree. Goodnight, sweet Angel, and goodnight Jason. I'll be retiring to my room. I'll make sure I'm up in time to make breakfast and get Angel ready for school."

"Thank you," Jason said. It was a simple statement, but Eliza felt the power in it. She could feel this man's gratitude already.

Eliza made her way back to the second floor. Once she got into her room, she flopped onto her bed. She had to make breakfast, and she didn't know the first thing about frying up bacon or serving omelets. She got up and flipped open her cell phone. She needed a little help, and Glory was just the person to give it.

"Just give them cereal, toast and orange juice. Surely, you can handle toast, Eliza," the older woman said, "I can't believe they let you get through angel school without any cooking classes."

"Yes, well none of my other assignments called for cooking if you recall. I suppose I'll have to make some sort of lunch for Jason and his mother tomorrow. Angel will be in school."

"You'll probably have to pack Angel's lunch don't forget," Glory gently reminded.

"Let's hope she likes peanut butter and jelly. Now what do I give Jason and his mother?"

"How about a bowl of chicken soup and a sandwich?"

"Fine. I guess I'll just have to play it by ear and see what they've got in the fridge. Thanks, Glory, and goodnight."

"Eliza, have you picked up any new feelings from Jason?"

"Yes," Eliza said thoughtfully, "I felt an overwhelming sense of gratitude and a powerful love for his daughter."

"Just wondering. Goodnight, Eliza. Call when you need help."

"That may be at seven tomorrow morning. Goodnight again," and Eliza clicked off her phone.

Eliza woke at six thirty so she could look through the pantry. Luckily the cabinets contained plenty of cereal. She set the table with two bowls and spoons and two small plates for the toast. She placed three boxes of cereal in the center of the table figuring they could choose what they wanted. She poured water into the coffee carafe and set it on the burner. Then, she put the coffee filter in and coffee beans. She felt a little flustered, but managed to pop four pieces of toast in the toaster and add jam to the items on the table. A minute later, she had the toast buttered and on the plates.

Eliza had her back turned, but she instantly sensed his presence before he even entered the room. She could feel a sense of calmness emanating from him.

"Good morning. Another early riser, I see."

"Yes, well I just want to learn my way around your kitchen. It is beautiful."

"I designed it myself. I'm glad you like it."

"Let me check on the coffee," Eliza went over to the coffee maker which she had switched on. She was perplexed. The water still sat in the carafe. No coffee. Jason appeared by her side.

"You forgot to put the water in the coffee maker."

"Oh," Eliza said not knowing where the water was exactly supposed to go.

"Here let me," Jason said taking over. Eliza watched as Jason took out the coffee beans. He smiled at her, "It helps if you grind them first."

"Oh," Eliza said again. She bit her bottom lip.

Jason ground the beans, poured the water and soon the coffee was perking.

"I'm not a coffee drinker, as you can tell."

Jason sensed her nervousness. "It's okay. We all do some things better than others. You've learned something new. Now maybe you'll start drinking it."

I hope cereal and toast is okay for this morning. I'll pour the orange juice."

"That's fine. I'll go wake Angel," Jason walked from the room to the staircase.

A couple minutes later, Jason returned with a sleepy-eyed Angel who looked like her name because of the halo of blonde curls. Angel did bed head beautifully.

"Hi, Eliza."

"Hi, Sweetie. What can I get for you?"

"I'll just have Rice Crispies."

Eliza poured the cereal in the bowl and added the milk. "Jam on your toast?"

"Yes, please."

Eliza quickly spread an adequate amount of jam on the bread. So far, so good.

"Eliza," Jason sounded abrupt, "I hope you plan on eating with us."

"No, I don't think it's the housekeeper's place to eat with the family."

"Not in my house. You're our caretaker, and you can expect to be treated like family. Please," he lowered his tone, "please join us."

Eliza figured it safer eating with them than preparing more food. She also felt something strange from Jason. She couldn't put her finger on it, but she knew this; he wanted her treated like family.

She poured herself a bowl of raisin bran. As she put jam on her toast she addressed Angel. "Honey, what would you like to take in your lunch?"

"Oh, you don't have to make her lunch. She buys the hot lunch at school everyday."

"Oh," Eliza let out a gush of air. *What a relief.*

After breakfast, Eliza ushered Angel back to her room to help her dress. "What would you like to wear today?"

"My blue uniform with a white blouse. I hate having to wear uniforms. We only get to wear three colors. In preschool I could wear anything I wanted. Daddy always made sure I had on a pretty dress and matching bow in my hair."

"Speaking of hair," Eliza held the coveted silver brush in her hand, "how would you like to wear it? In a pony tail?"

Angel shook her head. "No. Daddy likes it down. So do I. Except in the summer I sometimes like to wear it up."

"Well you look ready to me," Eliza stopped and stepped back, "You know, you really are a beautiful little girl. Inside and out," Angel's manners had not gone unnoticed by Eliza.

"Thank you," Angel said shyly, "I'd better go find Daddy."

"Let's look for him together. I don't know if he needs me to drop you off at school."

"Daddy's in his office," Angel said and led the way.

"Would you like me to drive her to school, Jason?" Eliza questioned as she peeked into his office.

"That won't be necessary. I'll be taking her to school, but it'll be a big help if you could pick her up every afternoon at two thirty."

"Fine," Eliza impulsively kissed the top of Angel's head, "Have a good day, and I'll see you later."

As Jason walked down the stairs, he stopped and looked back. "Will the movers be coming today?"

"Actually, I've rented a van. Like I said yesterday, I don't have much to move. I only rented the van on account of my harp being so large."

"Well, I'll be here to help you. All you have to do is knock on my office door whenever you need anything."

"Thank you. I'll see you later."

CHAPTER THREE

Jason helped Eliza carry the harp into her room. He couldn't believe how beautiful the instrument was. He'd never seen one up-close. They settled it into one corner, and Eliza quickly moved a chair behind it.

"There, that's perfect. Now all I have to do is unpack my bags and I'll be set."

"I want you to take your time, but I also hoped you could meet my Mom today."

"Why don't I go now? I'm eager to meet Vera, and I can always unpack later."

"You're sure?" Jason questioned.

"Absolutely," Eliza took a deep breath. She had no idea what to expect of Vera's condition. She knew first-hand how chemotherapy took its toll on people.

"Fine," Jason put his arm around Eliza and guided her to the door and across the hallway. Eliza instantly felt a sense of rightness. She shook her head. Her feelings were getting confused lately. She'd have to have a talk with the *Big Guy* one of these nights.

Jason knocked on the door.

"Come in," a weak voice answered. Jason opened the door, and

Eliza immediately got strong feelings of sorrow, but they weren't coming from Jason, they came from his mother.

"Mother, I'd like you to meet our new assistant, Eliza."

Vera smiled as she struggled to sit up in bed. "It's nice to meet you, dear."

"Eliza plays the harp so you'll be hearing some interesting music from across the hall."

Vera smiled and when she did, Eliza could immediately see the resemblance between mother and son. "Why I think that'll be lovely. Anything to cheer up the place. My son told you my condition's terminal?" Vera looked at her with concern. It seemed she felt she had to put Eliza at ease. Eliza knew most people didn't know how to react when told someone was dying; Ccurious to her and a strange human phenomenon. Sometimes it brought people closer, other times it made people feel uncomfortable and keep their distance. In this house, it brought people together, and that made Eliza glad. It would make her job a whole lot easier.

Eliza moved closer to the bed and lifted Vera's frail hand in hers. "Yes. Yes he did, and I'm here to help in any way I can. Maybe I can start by bringing you up something to eat?"

Vera sighed a heavy sigh, "I wish I could keep something down, but with this chemotherapy… I just don't keep my food down."

"When was the last time you had your therapy?"

"Yesterday. It's always worse the first few days after treatment. Eventually, my strength and appetite return, but then the cycle starts all over again."

Eliza knew she probably hadn't been out of bed much. "How about I sit and read to you for awhile. Oh, I know you can see well, but I just love reading aloud to people who'll listen."

Vera chuckled, "A showman… or woman should I say?"

"Yes, I have a bit of the theatrics in me. Anyway, it wouldn't be a bother unless you need your sleep."

"Oh, no. No more sleep. Please read to me."

Eliza turned to Jason. "I just have to get my book, I'll be right back."

Eliza darted across the hallway and shuffled through her bags. Finally she found the book she wanted to read: *Where Angels Walk*. She returned to Vera's room in time to catch Jason kissing his mother on the forehead.

"I'll leave you two to your reading." Jason made his way to the door.

"Jason?"

"Yes?"

"What would you and Angel like for dinner? I'll have to start it in a couple of hours."

"Why don't you ask Mom for one of her recipes and surprise us," with that, Jason gently closed the door.

"You know one of their favorite meals is Shepard's Pie."

Eliza didn't know if she was ready for this next step. "And how exactly does one go about making Shepard's Pie?"

Vera smiled. "It's actually quite easy. If you want to get a pen and paper from the desk over there, I'll give you the instructions."

Instructions. That's *exactly* what she needed to the nth degree. Eliza scanned the desk until she found a big notebook and pen. She came back to Vera's side and pulled over the wing back chair so that she could be closer to her.

"Well, you start by browning the hamburger. Make sure you drain the grease real good. Add some tomato sauce. Pat it down in a casserole dish. Then add any vegetables that you want. Jason and Angel love green beans and corn. Then top it off with mashed potatoes and bake for forty-five minutes at three hundred and seventy-five degrees. It's as simple as that."

Eliza thought it sounded pretty easy except she didn't know how to mash potatoes.

"Vera, how do you mash your potatoes? I know everyone does it differently," *there, a clever way of extracting information without sounding like a complete dunce.*

"Oh I cut my potatoes up real small before I drop them into the boiling water, and I boil them until they're very soft. Once they're drained, I add plenty of butter, some milk, and I'll give you my secret recipe that Jason and Angel just love; Add some garlic into the mix. Oh, and I never use the mixer. I always mash the potatoes with the hand masher. You'll find that in the silverware drawer."

"Thank you for that tip. I'll have to remember it. I only wish you could enjoy some."

"I will soon enough."

Eliza cocked an eyebrow knowing Vera wanted to continue on.

"Jason doesn't know it yet, but I've talked to my doctor and the people at hospice. I'm going to stop chemo. I want to die with dignity not with my head in the toilet bowl."

"I see," and Eliza did see. She agreed with Vera's decision one hundred percent. When her time was up God would take her, treatments or not. It was all in God's hands, but how would Jason handle that?

"Vera, do you believe in angels?"

The older woman thought about Eliza's question for a minute before answering. "I believe I have seen an angel. In my sleep," she waited to see Eliza's reaction before continuing, "She was beautiful, like you, and she helped me get to heaven to be with my husband and Mom and Dad."

"Do you believe God works in mysterious ways?"

"Yes, yes I do, but it's Jason who questions God's existence. Ever since his Kathleen was taken from him, he hasn't been the same. Thank heavens he had Angel to keep him from turning to drink or drugs or a lifestyle I wouldn't approve of. Angel kept him sane and respectable. She gave him a sense of purpose."

Eliza decided to approach the topic of sorrow since she felt an overwhelming amount of it coming through Vera. The reason she didn't know why. "Vera, why are you so sad? Because you have to leave your family behind? Or is there another reason?"

"You know, you're the first person to ask me that. I'm so confused. On one hand I'm happy because I'm going to be with my family again. On the other hand, I have to give up some family. It weighs heavily on my mind. It makes me sad because I'm confused. I don't know how I really should feel."

Eliza nodded. "I know what you mean about losing people you love. I miss my parents something awful. Years ago a car accident took their life. I was just a child. I really don't have anyone holding me here to earth like you. I just know I would be happy to go and be with my parents again."

"No boyfriend or husband?"

Eliza shook her head. "No. It's just me in this big world, but what does make me happy is taking care of the people I'm working for. I don't even look at it as work. It brings such joy to me to make someone happy."

Vera reached out her hand and patted Eliza's knee. "Poor child, no one to take care of you."

"Oh, don't feel sorry for me. My work fulfills my needs."

"Why don't you read that book you're holding about angels. I'd sure like to hear more about them."

So Eliza began reading accounts of real people believing they'd encountered angels in human form. One story particularly struck Vera. It was about a young boy out on a deserted road late at night and caught in a fierce snowstorm. The weather so bad he got stuck, but with no cars in sight, he gave up hope. At that moment his heater decided to break. He expected to freeze to death. Out of nowhere came a car with a man and a woman who helped him move his car so that he could travel again. He turned around to thank them, but they were gone. He couldn't imagine where they had disappeared to so fast. In his heart, he believed God had sent him angels to help him on his way.

A tear trickled down Vera's cheek. Instinctively, Eliza reached out to wipe it. "Quite some story isn't it?" Eliza said, gently.

"You know what I think, Eliza? God sent you to help me and my family. So, I guess you're our angel."

Eliza didn't know what to say. So, she leaned in and whispered to Vera. "Can you keep a secret?"

Vera nodded.

"I can't cook for diddlysquat, but Jason doesn't know it, and I'm not sure how I'm going to bungle my way through that part of my job."

Vera smiled, and it reached her eyes. "Well, then I'll just have to help you, dear. It'll be good feeling like I'm still useful. I'll give you cooking lesson from my bed. It will be our secret."

Eliza knew she made the right decision in admitting she couldn't cook. Not only would it help Vera, but it would help her. See. *The Big Guy knew I didn't need cooking lessons going through angel school because he must have known I'd get them from Vera.* She couldn't wait to tell Glory.

After reading Vera a few more stories, the woman who looked so fragile against the stark white sheets and pillowcase, fell asleep. Eliza quietly left the room and headed straight for the kitchen.

"Glory, I'm getting cooking lessons at long last," Eliza said into the small phone as she paced back and forth in the gourmet style kitchen with the shiny copper pots hanging overhead.

"Well, I'm glad to see things are working out. Just always remember, Eliza, you've got God on your side, and God always has a plan."

"Thanks for the reminder, but Vera helps me see God in different ways."

"Which may be the reason for this assignment. There's always a lesson to be learned... a purpose to be served."

"Gotta go make some Shepard's Pie. Talk soon," and Eliza flipped off her cell phone. "Okay, I need potatoes and a peeler," Eliza had a vague memory of her mother peeling potatoes every night for dinner. It made her long for home. Oh, she just had to do this assignment just right so she could see her mother and father one more time. Glory didn't say if it was just a visit or a permanent thing, but either made her happy.

Eliza furiously peeled potatoes. That's how Jason found her. He knocked on the doorway.

"Hello. I don't mean to interrupt, but I just thought I'd grab something to hold me over until dinner."

"Oh no," Eliza slapped her hand to her forehead, "I forgot your lunch. I got so caught up with your Mom… I'm sorry. It won't happen again."

Jason approached her slowly and then pulled a potato peel from a long blonde curl. "It's okay. I'd much rather you focus your attention on my mother. In fact, I really didn't feel hungry up until now. I'll just grab a ham sandwich and go back to work, but what time is dinner?"

Eliza looked at her watch. It said two fifteen. "My goodness, I best be going for Angel."

"Don't worry," Jason soothed, "It's only a five minute drive. You have plenty of time," he realized Eliza was trying to get adjusted to her new schedule.

Eliza threw down her apron and picked up her car keys and purse. She quickly threw on her coat. "Dinner will be at five, and I'll have Angel home shortly," she hurried out the front door and into her Honda Accord.

Eliza waved her hands at Angel. "Over here," she said. Angel spotted her new nanny and came running. The man standing next to Eliza introduced himself.

"I'm Bill Wiggins. My daughter is in the same grade as Angel."

"Yes, well, I'm Angel's new… nanny."

Bill extended his hand. "Nice to meet you—"

"Eliza."

"Eliza. I'll talk to you tomorrow."

Eliza guided Angel back to the car. She got strong feelings of attraction from Bill Wiggins. If she could read him right, he wanted to ask her on a date. No time for human dating. She had a job to do.

The minute Angel burst through the doors, she ran right into her father's open arms. "Oh, Daddy, Daddy, I've missed you so."

"I know Angel Baby, I've missed you, too."

Eliza didn't know what to do right at that moment since this was all new to her, so she asked. "Does Angel have homework she needs help with?"

Angel laughed. "Oh no, thank God. I'm only in Kindergarten. We don't get homework until next year. I get to play now."

"Hmmm," Eliza said, "How would you like to help me make a surprise dinner for your Dad instead?"

"Really? You really want me to help?" Angel almost bounced out of the room.

"Only if you want to."

"Daddy, can I?"

Jason looked at Eliza. Something about her made him feel totally secure in leaving his mother and child in her hands. He couldn't explain it, but he hadn't felt that way in a long, long time. Not since Kathleen…

"So now I can pour in the green beans and corn?"

Eliza nodded.

"What's next?"

"Now we cover the whole mess with a big lump of mashed potatoes."

"Goody. I can drop them on top," Angel said as she scooped up some of the potatoes Eliza had mashed in the big pot, "I can't wait until Daddy sees. He loves Shepard's Pie as much as I do. It'll be such a surprise. And I helped."

"You certainly did. You'd make a wonderful Girl Scout," Eliza said without thinking.

Angel crunched up her eyebrows. "What do you mean?"

Eliza sensed anger in Angel so she backed off. "Nothing, honey, expect that you're going to be a good cook."

"Good. Because I'm not going to ever be a Girl Scout. Not as long as Emily Watson is one. She's mean."

Now Eliza started to read Angel's feelings better. The anger was directed at this girl Angel didn't like—not at Eliza. It made Eliza feel grateful.

"Okay, now all we have to do is pop this in the oven and wait. What do you want to do while we wait?"

"Well, can I get out of my uniform?"

"Certainly," Eliza hadn't even realized she hadn't changed the child.

"Then can I visit with grandma?"

"She was sleeping, sweetheart, last time I saw her, but if she's awake, I'm sure she'll want to see you as much as you want to see her."

Eliza and Angel made their way up to Angel's bedroom. Angel pulled out a pair of jeans and a sweatshirt that read *God's Watching Over Me.*

"What a great sweatshirt, Angel. Did you pick it out?"

"No," Angel said sadly, "Grandma did when she was better. She always tells me God is watching over me. Why does God take people you love away from you, Eliza?" the innocence and wonder of her question struck a chord in Eliza's heart. The wonder part Eliza understood completely.

"Because God misses his children, too, Angel. You're one of his children, and he'd like to visit with you, too."

"Then why can't we come back and be like a family again. Why can't my Mommy be finished with her visit and come back?"

"That, I don't know, Angel," she spoke the truth. Eliza didn't know why God did the things he did. She just knew he had his reasons for everything. If she didn't believe that she'd still be mourning her parents instead of helping someone else on earth. Now she had hope that she'd see them again someday, so she decided to pass this positive thought onto Angel. "I'm sure God will let you be with your Mom again, one day."

"Really? Do you really think God will let me be with my mother again?" Angel's face lit up.

"Yes, Angel, it will happen. God knows what's important to us. But know that you have a purpose on this earth. There's a reason why you're alive."

"Sometimes I wonder what it's all about," Angel said with a dejected sigh.

Eliza understood her feelings exactly. "Angel, Honey, it's about so much more. God has a big, big plan in effect. You and I are just a small part of it. But know one thing. You are meant to carry out your life here on earth.

"Maybe I'll grow up to be like you and help other people. Eliza…"

Angel paused, "sometimes I dream bad things."

"What kind of bad things, Sweetie?" Now Eliza felt she'd hit the heart of it.

"That the devil takes my Mommy away from heaven."

"I can guarantee you this, Angel. God is far more powerful than any devil and your mother is safe in heaven. Besides, there really is no devil."

Angel screwed up her little face. "But, at school they teach us all about him."

"Well, I think the devil is like monsters. He doesn't exist. It's just a way to scare people into being good."

Angel seemed to contemplate it. "I also dream my Daddy dies, and I have nobody to take care of me."

Eliza embraced Angel. "Oh, Sweetheart. No one knows when they're going to die, but I don't think your Daddy is going anywhere for a long, long time."

"Do you really believe that?"

"With my whole heart and soul. Maybe," Eliza worded her next sentence carefully, "some day your Dad will meet another woman and get married. Then you'd have a step Mommy. Would you like that?"

Angel nodded. "But, she'd never be my real Mommy."

"No, Angel, she'd never take the place of your real Mommy, but maybe it would be just another person who'd love you and take care of you and your Dad."

"I think Daddy needs someone like that... to take care of him," Angel bit her fingernails.

"Why do you say that, Angel?"

"Because he's all alone at night, and I've heard him crying. That's why I sleep with him because of that and my bad dreams."

"I think your Daddy will find someone in time, but Honey, I think he can sleep alone. Everyone needs a good cry. It's okay to cry when you're sad, but about those bad dreams... we're going to chase them away with prayers."

"What do you mean?" Angel asked.

"When you're ready to sleep in your own bed again, I'll tell you. Deal?"

"Deal," Angel held up her pinky, and Eliza wrapped hers around Angel's just like she'd seen Jason do.

"Eliza," Angel hesitated.

Eliza waited patiently. "Yes?"

"Sometimes I dream that I die and go to heaven to be with my Mommy."

"Maybe, it's just your Mommy's way of telling you she's okay and that the two of you will be reunited someday when the time is right."

Angel threw her arms around Eliza. "I wish you could be my step Mommy," she whispered into her ear.

Eliza squeezed her hard. Oh, how she would love to take care of this precious child forever.

"Would you like to be my step Mommy?" an innocent Angel asked.

Eliza didn't want to hurt the little girl's feelings, so she simply said, "Yes, but I can't. Your Daddy will find a wife one day," a tear slid down Eliza's cheek. She didn't know why, but she felt such powerful emotions and the incredible unconditional love of this special child. She quickly wiped the tear before letting go of Angel. She didn't want her to see her crying. She had to pull herself together.

CHAPTER FOUR

Eliza never expected Angel to open up to her so much. Well, finding Jason and Angel a new wife and Mommy had to take top priority. If this was be her last assignment, maybe not, she'd make sure both of them were capable of living full, happy, productive lives.

"Why don't we go check on dinner. I think your father's going to be very surprised his little girl can cook so good."

"Oh, Eliza. You did most of the work."

"No, Angel, you did as much as I did. Let's go," she held out her hand to the tiny six-year-old girl.

Just then, Eliza had mixed emotions from Angel, but she knew one thing. Angel became more attached to her by the moment. Good on one hand. Not so good once she had to go. She'd have to talk to Glory about this situation. Eliza and Angel made their way into the deluxe designer kitchen. Its size and organization still impressed Eliza. There were white cabinets everywhere and some with glass doors just jumped out at you. She and Angel peeked into the stove and saw a most promising sight. The potatoes were a golden brown.

"Well, Angel Baby, I think dinner is ready. Want to help set the table?"

"Sure, Eliza. You know you're the only one to call me Angel Baby besides my Mommy and Daddy."

"I won't if you don't like it."

Angel looked pensive for a moment before saying, "No, I like it a lot."

Eliza let Angel lead her to her father's office on the third floor. All of its shiny cherry hardwood floors and walls made it a sight to behold. Angel knocked on the door, and her father came out. He immediately embraced his little girl.

"So, how was school today? Get into any trouble?" he smiled.

"Oh, Daddy, like I ever do anything to get into trouble."

Jason ruffled the top of her blonde curly head.

Jason looked up at Eliza and couldn't help but notice her blue eyes. She had the most beautiful, expressive eyes he'd ever seen. This marked the first time in a long time that he noticed a woman's eyes, and it shocked him.

"Dinner's ready, Jason, and it's a surprise that both Angel and me worked on. Would you like to see it?"

Jason looked from Eliza to his daughter. "Absolutely. Let me finish up one last thing and then I'll wash my hands and be down for dinner," to Eliza, he said, "How's my Mom doing?"

"I checked on her on the way up. She's sound asleep."

"Good. At least she's not in pain when she sleeps. At least not so far."

Five minutes later, Jason joined Eliza and Angel at the table. He was surprised by his special dinner.

"I didn't think anyone could make Shepard's Pie as good as my Mom, but Angel, you and Eliza did a great job. It's just as good—if not better than grandma's. Just don't tell her. That's our secret."

Dinner went by quickly. Jason let Eliza clean up while he helped Angel with some of her learning books. Then, Eliza poked her head in the room with the Christmas tree, the living room, and announced she could now play with Angel. Jason seemed relieved.

"I can't thank you enough for coming into our lives. You just don't know what this means to me," Jason said.

"What if I told you I understand exactly what it means?"

"Then, you're an angel who knows my every thought."

Eliza laughed. "Expect to hear this angel on her harp early this evening. I'm going to bring Angel along before her bedtime. Is that all right?"

"Of course. I think it's a good thing to expose children to the arts at an early age."

Jason finished up his work when he heard the first few strains from the harp. The soft, beautiful music reached his ear and made him feel something different, and something settling at that. It disappointed him when it finally stopped.

"Oh, Eliza. I would love to play the harp like you. Will you give me lessons? Will you?"

"It's easy to learn if you just follow your heart, but now it's time for bed. Let's go to your father's office and remind him he has a story to read tonight."

Angel smiled. "I like you. You make me happy. I really wish you could be my step Mommy."

That statement threw Eliza even though it hadn't been the first time she'd heard it that day. She, too, started to feel awfully attached to this sweet, precious child. Her father? A story unto its own. Yes, she admitted to herself that Jason... how did she find him? awfully handsome? But, that's not what bothered Eliza. If she had to describe Jason it meant saying a good man trying to care for the two people left in this world to care for. She felt his need for more. She felt his attraction to her, and that surprised her because she thought Kathleen would always take precedence over any other. Now, she realized how wrong her thinking was. Jason Abbott needed another wife, and she feared he believed her the solution to his problems. Her feelings told her that, and that *Big Guy Upstairs* is the one who let her in on these little secrets. What she didn't understand is why he would give her an assignment where she'd be tempted to stray.

"Daddy, Daddy, I'm going to learn how to play the harp. Did you hear Eliza? She plays beautiful music. I want to play like that one day, and Eliza said she could teach me if I follow my heart."

"Is that what she said? Follow your heart, and the rest will follow. That's what your mother always used to say to me. I think Eliza is on to something."

"Here she is, Daddy," Angel dragged Eliza into the room behind her.

"I only want her to learn… "

Jason immediately cut her off. "If she wishes to learn any musical instrument, let me know. I'm only too happy to make my daughter happy."

"Well, it seems like it's the harp for her, Daddy. Can you accept that?"

"Absolutely. I heard that music and know it's from someone very talented, and I'm betting my mother is still awake wondering about your music. Would you see to my mother while I take Angel to bed for her bedtime story?"

"Absolutely, Jason," she turned to Angel and kissed her on the cheek, "Sweet dreams, my love. I'll see you in the morning."

CHAPTER FIVE

Jason couldn't believe what he felt. In the years since his wife's death, he never looked at another female. It seemed to be a wake-up call. With Eliza everything seemed different. His attraction to her as a woman as well as a man in need of a child care taker over ruled all other senses. More importantly, she made him put things in perspective. He knew he'd never have Kathleen back, but could he, could he possibly have someone else to love in this lifetime? He let those thoughts flow through his mind and decided to visit his mother after Angel fell asleep and Eliza finished her visit with Vera. Somehow, his mother always knew what bothered him.

An hour later, he knocked on the door twice, and then heard her weak reply to enter. What he saw scared him to death. His mother looked so pale and frightfully thin. He didn't think anything could help her.

Vera felt glad for this private moment with her son. She had gone ahead with her chemotherapy, but now, for certain, she would not continue no matter what anyone said.

"Do you like seeing me this way, Jason?" Vera managed to whisper.

"Of course not, Mother. You know better than that."

"Then, let me stop the chemo treatments and let me die with dignity. I want to eat the foods I want to eat. I want to walk and not feel confined to a bed. I want to be free as long as our Good Lord will let me be free."

Jason hadn't expected Vera's strong words, but as he watched her throw up in a garbage can, he decided, the final days of her life were up to her. "I support any decision you make, Mom. I only want you around for many, many years."

"That's not always possible, Jason. Sometimes, God calls us home early for different reasons. Please, let me join you and Angel and Eliza in dinners and happy events. Once I'm off chemo, I'll be so much stronger. I can at least be a real part of your lives for awhile.

It took three weeks before Vera could walk on her own. She smiled at Eliza. "You won't be holding me much sooner. I feel myself getting stronger every day. Eliza, I just want my son and grandbaby to remember me with positive thoughts—not thoughts of me sick and weak and unable to communicate."

Eliza smiled back. "I agree with your decision, Vera, though I don't know what Jason thinks just yet, but you stick to your guns. I believe you're on the right track. When God is ready to take you, he will no matter what."

Vera decided to pursue a subject she'd been wondering about. "You said you can't cook for diddlysquat. How did you get this job then? My son believes in having a cook in the house?"

"Can we say its just destiny that I should be taking care of you and Angel and Jason. That doesn't mean I'm perfect, especially in the cooking department, but you got me covered there. Right?"

Eliza sounded nervous. She feared Vera would reveal their secret. "No, Eliza. I plan on helping you with every meal that's made, now that I'm gaining strength."

"The one reason your son hired me… I said I could cook. I can't Vera. Not for the life of me."

"So you said. Well, I'm still willing to teach, if you're willing to learn. And Jason doesn't have to know," she winked, "Every good woman has her secrets, but nothing we can't fix."

Things next morning meant changes. Vera worked hard at the stove mixing together omelets she knew her son and granddaughter would like. Quickly Vera ordered Eliza to put four pieces of toast in the toaster and boil water for tea.

Someone else in charge of the kitchen left Eliza relieved. "Do you think they need a small bowl of cereal as well? Eliza asked the elderly lady. Vera just laughed a small laugh and told Eliza she knew her son and grandbaby would be plenty full after this breakfast, and she told Eliza she should take credit for the work.

Eliza immediately protested, but Vera made her promise she would take credit for the breakfast on the table, and she also promised to show her how, in private, to make the same breakfast. So, when Jason and Angel came down to breakfast, they were surprised to have such a wonderful feast.

"This is absolutely fantastic, Eliza," Jason said as he shoveled another forkful into his mouth.

"Just like grandma's," Angel added.

Vera winked across the table at Eliza.

"Yes, well I aim to please," Eliza nervously twisted the kitchen towel in her hand.

"Please join us, Eliza," Jason had stopped eating to make his request. Eliza complied. She flipped the last omelet onto her dish and poured herself some freshly squeezed orange juice.

"I can't tell you how good it is to have you join us, Mom," Jason directed to his mother dressed in a housecoat for a change.

"Well, I'm feeling much better, and Eliza has promised to wash and set my hair today so that I don't look like a witch."

"Oh, Grandma, you're so funny. You don't look like a witch," Angel said as she bit into a piece of toast.

"Well, I plan on being up and around here for awhile."

Jason finished the last of his food and put the dish and utensils into the dishwasher. "Time to go to school, Angel Baby," Jason tugged on a blonde pigtail that Angel had insisted Eliza do despite the fact it wasn't summer.

Angel scrambled. She followed her father's example and put her dishes into the dishwasher. Then, she gave Eliza a quick kiss on the cheek. She dashed over to her grandmother and gave her a big bear hug. "Maybe we can play Old Maid when I come home from school?"

"Count on it. I'll take my nap early so that we can enjoy a game or two. Now, scat little Angel. I love you."

"I love you, too, Grandma," Angel skipped down the hall to join her father. Once Jason pulled out of the drive way, Vera stood very slowly. "I think the cooking lesson will have to wait a couple of hours. I'm feeling a bit tired, Eliza, dear."

Eliza immediately laced her arm through Vera's. "Let me help you upstairs. We'll get you settled, and when you're feeling better we'll do your hair and nails."

Vera stopped half way up the stairs. "Just need a breather is all, but I'll be honest with you. I feel much better now that I'm not going through that awful chemotherapy."

"Well, you had a busy morning. I'd say you're doing just fine," they started to climb the stairs again. When Vera reached the bed she just plunked herself down. Eliza slipped off Vera's slippers and swung her legs so they were on the bed. She fluffed Vera's pillow. "Is there anything else I can do for you?" she asked, concern written all over her face.

"Just wake me for lunch. Do you think you can manage ham sandwiches and Campbells soup?" Vera smiled.

Eliza laughed. "That I can do. I'll serve Jason in his office, and I'll bring yours up here."

"Once I get stronger, I'll be teaching you how to make all sorts of fancy lunches, but for today, I think breakfast was enough."

Eliza leaned over and planted a kiss on Vera's forehead the same way she had witnessed her son do the day before.

"You know, if I had to have a second daughter-in-law, it would be you."

Eliza blushed only because she was starting to find herself looking at Jason in a manly way. "Well, that's quite the compliment, but I think I like being your angel best."

Vera's eyes fluttered and closed. Eliza tip-toed out the door and gently pulled it shut. She jumped when she felt a hand on her shoulder.

"I'm sorry. I didn't mean to scare you. I just wanted to talk to you about my mother. How is she doing?"

"She's sleeping now, but I'll have her gussied up for dinner. I'm going to do her hair and nails. You know, one of the first things they teach you about terminal patients is to keep them feeling normal, not to let themselves go. I know when I'm sick, I can't wait to wash my hair."

Jason just nodded. "She seemed so much better at breakfast. She hasn't been this good in a long while. Maybe stopping the chemo is for the best."

"I know it's not my place to say this, Jason, but God will take your mother when he's good and ready, chemo or not. That's my belief anyway."

"Thank you for taking such good care of her."

Eliza felt a strong pulling from Jason, almost as though he wanted to hug her. "It's my job, Jason. But truth is, I'd do it no matter what. She's a wonderful woman, and I'll do everything I can to make her comfortable."

"Thank you... Eliza," Jason turned to leave then, as an afterthought, turned back. "What's for dinner?" he smiled, and Eliza caught her breath.

"I'm not sure. I'll see what recipe you're Mom will pass on to me."

"You're a mighty good cook, and I'll be looking forward to some more of your harp playing this evening. You will be playing won't you?"

Eliza blushed. She never did that around men. Why now? Oh God. *Yep, Big Guy Upstairs, why am I feeling these strange feelings?* "I will if you, Angel and Vera want."

"I'm sure they'll appreciate it too."

"Then, my concert is tonight, sir." Eliza affected a bow.

Jason laughed. "Did you ever consider playing with the local Philharmonic?"

"No, I just play for my own pleasure. It gives me a sense of peace when I play."

"We all need some kind of outlet."

"What's yours?" it popped out of Eliza's mouth before she could stop it.

"Basketball. Did you notice the hoop in the driveway. That's not for Angel, though she's always welcome to play. No, it's for me when I have to burn off some steam, when things get too crazy. It relieves my stress, but who knows, maybe Angel will want to learn one day."

"I'd like to see you play," Eliza said.

Jason swallowed. For some reason he found this conversation turning more intimate than planned. However he welcomed it and didn't know why. "I'd be happy to show you a couple of moves, just don't expect to teach me how to play the harp in return," he said in jest.

"Deal," Eliza watched as Jason climbed the steps to the third floor.

Looked like this angel wasn't only going to learn how to cook. Eliza slipped into her room and called Glory. She needed some grounding, and fast.

"Vera's doing much better now that she's stopped that dreadful chemotherapy. By the time I finish here I should be a world class chef and star basketball player," she joked into the phone.

Glory laughed. "You can always use everything you learn. You'll see. How are your relationships with the family going?"

"Vera is a lot like my grandmother. She's taken me under her wing. Angel's like the daughter I never had, and Jason… he's quite the gentleman."

"But, what's his relationship with you like?" a curious Glory asked. She knew her student and knew something was up.

"It's becoming a nice friendship," *well that is the truth*, Eliza told herself. She didn't feel comfortable yet telling Glory her attraction to Jason as a man.

"Good. And remember, Eliza, that's all you and Jason can ever be if you want to see your parents again."

That immediately stopped all thoughts of Jason as anything other than an employer and friend. Thank God she'd called Glory. Now she knew the score. She couldn't become involved with Jason or she'd never see her parents.

CHAPTER SIX

"Oh, Grandma! Grandma! You look beautiful," Angel said as soon as she burst through the front door. She launched herself into her grandmother's arms.

Vera chuckled. "See what a little make-up magic can do."

"You look great, Mom," Jason said. He looked over at Eliza, "Looks like you have other talents, too."

"Oh, I just like to play hairdresser, make-up artist and dress up. I have to admit, I had a wonderful client," Eliza slipped her arm through Vera's.

Jason watched the exchange between his mother and Eliza. They quickly became friends, and he quickly got used to having Eliza around. For a brief moment, he wondered what it would be like to kiss her. Would she taste as good as she looked? And how would she feel about kissing him? He stopped his train of thought. Their relationship remained that of employer and employee and maybe friend, but if honest with himself, he'd have to admit she attracted him like no other since… Kathleen. Not only did she get along wonderfully with his family, but she was truly a beautiful woman. A picture of Kathleen flew through his mind. No, he'd have to honor his dedication to his deceased wife. With her went all chances of dating other women.

He'd made that promise to Kathleen, and he intended to keep it. Never mind that Kathleen made him promise to remarry after she passed on. She'd told him that Angel would need a mother and he a wife. At the time, his grief so unbearable, he couldn't even imagine what being with any other woman but Kathleen would be like.

Now, Eliza entered their lives. They say God works in mysterious ways. He'd have to sit and ponder that.

Vera broke into his thoughts. "How about that game of Old Maid my little Angel?"

"Goody! I'll go get my cards. We can play in the kitchen while Eliza makes dinner."

Vera gave Eliza a quick look. "No, I think we should play in my room. Then, when we're done you can practice some of those study books your Daddy gave you."

"Okay," Angel seemed agreeable enough.

Eliza let out a sigh of relief. Once Angel was gone, Eliza turned to Vera, "What are we making for dinner tonight?"

"Chicken and peppers. They both adore that dish, and it's as simple as can be. Just reach into that cabinet and pull out two jars of pepper salad."

Eliza did as told.

"Now, get the Italian breadcrumbs and olive oil, and we can't forget to thaw out the chicken cutlets."

Eliza's head was spinning. Maybe she wasn't cut out to be a cook. Eventually she found everything and placed each item on the counter.

"Now you just leave everything there, and I'll be down right after I finish playing with my granddaughter. Would you mind helping me upstairs?"

Eliza jumped to her side in an instant. "Of course not, and I have to agree with Jason and Angel, you look like a real knock out."

Vera just gave Eliza a look that said *right*.

"For someone my age… maybe."

They found Angel bouncing on the bed with a deck of cards in her hands.

"I'll leave you two be. Angel, come tell me when your grandmother wants to come back down into the kitchen."

"Okay. Grandma, can I shuffle the deck?"

"You sure can young lady."

Eliza slipped out the door. She looked up the stairs that led to the third floor and Jason's office. She knew he usually took care of his own lunch, but something was pushing her to go to him. So, she quietly made her way up the steps. When she reached Jason's office door she heard his voice loud and clear. "Jeff, I don't want to double date. I told you before. I don't want to date. Period. So, please leave it be."

Eliza could only guess what the man named Jeff on the other line said by Jason's reaction.

"Thank you for respecting my wishes. I know you're only trying to help. But... I still think about Kathleen. It's too hard right now, Jeff. Okay. Good-bye."

Eliza felt like an eavesdropper, but she didn't want to barge in on him while he finished his conversation. She took a deep breath and knocked on the door.

"Come in," Jason said in his usual pleasant voice, but he seemed a bit flustered. He wondered if Eliza had overheard his conversation with Jeff.

"I just dropped your mother off in her room. She and Angel are playing cards, so I thought I'd come up here and see if I could make you a sandwich for lunch?"

Jason noticed how Eliza's Christmas sweater fit her so nicely showing off all of her womanly curves. Once again, he found himself thinking wayward thoughts. He shook his head. "Sure, that would be great. I'm not fussy so surprise me."

"I'll be back shortly," Eliza said as she slowly backed up. Jason made her nervous. She definitely read some powerful vibes and they weren't all platonic. It confused her because of the conversation she'd just overheard. She bumped into the door and said, "Oops! I'm so clumsy. Let's hope I don't drop your sandwich on the way up," then she opened the door and quickly disappeared down the steps.

When she got to the kitchen, she opened the refrigerator. She knew exactly what she wanted to make him. God only knew why, but for some reason she knew how to make a dynamite Italian sub. She quickly gathered the meats and cheeses, lettuce and tomatoes. She whipped up the dressing. Before she knew it, the finished product sat in front of her looking perfectly edible. She had reason to be proud of herself. Now, if she could only control her thoughts when she went to deliver said lunch.

This time Jason wasn't on the phone, and he smiled when he saw what she'd brought him. She even remembered he liked diet soda.

"Well, something looks good enough to eat."

The pause lingered and the two just looked at each other. An uncomfortable silence followed. Eliza spoke first. "I better get back in the kitchen so I can work on dinner. It's another one of your mother's recipes, so I'm sure you'll like it."

"Don't tell me. Surprise me."

Eliza turned to go when Jason said, "Eliza, there's been something I've been wanting to tell you. You're more than welcome to invite your boyfriend here for visits or dinner."

Eliza swallowed hard. "Thank you. I'll keep that in mind," she turned and practically ran out the door. Confused by her feelings, she wondered why. Why did it upset her that Jason wanted her with another man, and why didn't she tell him there wasn't one. Because she didn't want him to think her interested in him any way other than friend and employer. Oh what, oh what, could she tell Glory when she asked about her feelings for Jason? She knew her place as an angel for heaven's sake, and Jason? Human male. Human. Albeit an incredibly good-looking one. She also liked the vibes she got around him when he spent time with his mother and daughter. He treated them so well, and Eliza thought him too good to be true in this day and age.

As she hit the second floor landing, Angel, came bounding out of her grandmother's room. "Grandma said she's ready to go downstairs, and I'm going to work on my study books in my room."

Good, Eliza thought. It's the first step to getting her to sleep in her own room.

51

Vera smiled and Eliza felt the warm welcome this woman had for her. The genuine warmth and realness of it felt so good to have someone like her care for her.

"Ready to go on our secret mission?" Eliza whispered.

Vera laughed. I'm feeling much better, so let's go.

On the way down, Eliza felt tempted to tell Vera what Angel had told her about why she slept with her father. She decided Angel might not want her to know, and it not her place to tell.

Once they got in the kitchen, Vera worked like a whirlwind. "See, the key here is using lots of olive oil," she let that cook in the frying pan while she dipped the chicken cutlets in milk and Italian bread seasoning. Then she tossed everything into the fry pan. Once everything was brown, she put the chicken into a big casserole dish. "Here's the secret ingredient, Eliza."

Eliza just nodded not knowing if she could replicate this dinner.

"Pepper salad," Vera proceeded to dump the two jars into the casserole dish and added a little olive oil and water. "Now, we just leave it in the oven for one hour at 350. Maybe a little less. We'll just have to check on it. Let's sit and we'll chat."

Eliza obeyed. "You sure are a whiz in the kitchen."

"You'll get the hang of it in no time. I think you're going to be a fine student, and that coming from a retired school teacher is quite a compliment."

"So you were a teacher? Of what?"

"Third grade Math. That's where Jason gets all his common sense. What did you do before this?" Vera asked in a way that let Eliza know she wasn't being nosey, just curious.

"Well, I worked for a family with a ten-year-old boy dying of bone cancer. I only spent a few months before he… before he passed on," Eliza's eyes filled as she recalled Davey's last words to her, "You're my angel."

"I'm sorry to hear that. It's a pity when someone so young is taken from this earth. Me? I've had a good life. I love my son and granddaughter in a way I can't describe, but like I told you, I miss my husband and Mom and Dad."

As soon as Vera mentioned missing her Mom and Dad a bell went off. If she let her feelings for Jason and Angel get out of control, she wouldn't see her parents. Oh, what she wouldn't give to have her mom and dad's arms around her in a big bear hug. It seemed like only yesterday she spent her time with them. She grew up in the angel's side of heaven. She always marveled at how only adults could be angels. So, children trained from the day they entered that side of heaven. She didn't know why she was chosen to be an angel because all children and adults weren't – like her parents. Glory had only said that her mother and father had done everything right in their last life so they would be together for eternity. They never had to come back down to earth. Many, many souls didn't find that the case. They came back down to, as Glory said, "get it right."

"I know what you mean about missing your Mom and Dad. I think about mine a lot. You know, the things I've missed out on. The only thing that makes me feel better is knowing that they're with God."

"You have a strong belief in God, don't you, Eliza?"

"Oh yes. I believe there is a *Big Guy Upstairs* looking out for all of us. And I believe he sends out his angels to do his work."

"Interesting. You'd think someone all alone in this world might be bitter or not believe He answered their prayers."

"Vera, when you work with people the way I do, you get a sense of satisfaction. You also see how prayers are answered. They're not always the answers we want, but there's a reason for everything. You know, I had one client pray that he win a trip to California. Well, when he didn't win, he thought God wasn't answering his prayers. As it turned out, the flight he would have been on, crashed. Every single person was killed. In my mind, God told him he wasn't ready for him yet by not answering his prayer the way he wanted."

"The only thing you're missing in your life, Child, is a husband and children."

"I've pretty much ruled that out. Besides, if I did have a husband and children, I couldn't do as much work as I do now."

"You really are God's helper. You know, when Jason was younger and Kathleen was alive, there wasn't a Sunday that would go by that they didn't go to mass. Jason always said it's about finding your soul mate, but I never believed Kathleen was his. Oh sure, he loved her with all his being. Kathleen was more his friend than a wife if you know what I mean."

"I think I do," to herself she thought, *any man who weeps at night for his lost love has found his soul mate.* "Do you think your husband is your soul mate?"

Vera looked out the kitchen window for a moment before replying, "I do. Henry was a good man, and I know I'm on my way to joining him in heaven. Don't ask me how I know that. I just do. My heart tells me what I need to know."

"Aren't you afraid of dying, Vera?" Eliza asked gently.

"Oh, no dear. If I didn't know about heaven, I might be. My dreams sometimes seem so real. I told you about the angel in my dream… the one who takes me to my Henry. I've also dreamed that Henry is telling me he's waiting for me, and it won't be long before we're together again."

A tear slid down Eliza's face. She would miss Vera. That was the hardest part of her job. She was always saying good-bye to the people she came to love.

"Why the tear, Child?" Vera covered her older, more wrinkled hand over Eliza's hand.

"I'm just thinking how much I'll miss you."

Vera chuckled. "Tell you what. I'll come to you in your dreams and give you cooking lessons. You're going to need them if you stay here with my son."

Eliza looked up, and that's when Vera knew. Eliza had fallen for her son.

"Why of course. Every good nanny needs to know how to cook. I've just never had to in any of my other jobs, and my mother wasn't around to show me."

"Well, I'm proud as a peacock to be the one teaching you my recipes. It's good to know they'll live on after I'm gone. It'll make Jason feel more…" Vera couldn't find the word she looked for.

"More at home?"

"Yes," Vera shook her head, "More secure."

They talked for the next forty-five minutes uninterrupted. They talked about everything. Vera told Eliza about the days as a younger girls she used to go to the candy store down the street from her old house and buy two pieces of candy for a penny. She told her about having an outhouse in her early years. About the ice man and the milk man. She even told Eliza of her family tree. The buzzer rang.

"Let's go see what we've concocted. Shall we?" Vera said as she slowly raised herself from the chair.

"Here, let me help you," Eliza found herself at her side in a flash. Together they went to the oven. Vera slipped on an oven mitt and pulled the chicken dish out. It was still bubbling.

"My, that smells wonderful," Eliza said as her stomach rumbled.

"Wait until you taste it, my dear. Go get some instant white rice from the cabinet."

Eliza did as she was told.

"Now here's how you make fluffy white rice. You follow the directions on the box exactly. Three cups of water to a boil, and then add three cups of rice. Remove from heat and let sit for five minutes. Go ahead. You try it. We serve this dish over rice."

Eliza followed the instructions and ten minutes later she had a pot of fluffy white rice. She was just about to kiss Vera on the cheek and thank her when she felt him. He had been watching them. She felt Jason's heart skip a beat when she turned around.

"What are two of my favorite ladies up to?"

"Oh, you're mother's just..."

"Just marveling over what a wonderful job Eliza did with my recipe," Vera interrupted.

"I smelled it all the way upstairs and had to come down. Chicken and peppers are another one of our favorites as I'm sure my Mom has told you."

"Yes, well, maybe we should get Angel and sit down to eat while it's still hot."

Jason looked into Eliza's eyes, and she felt like he could see her heart much the same way she could see his. But that was foolish. She, an angel with extra sensitive perceptions? He couldn't possibly know what she'd been thinking, but she knew someone who could. The Chief. She promised herself tonight she'd have a talk with him.

"I'll be back in a jiffy."

Eliza watched as Jason walked down the hall. She noticed not for the first time what broad shoulders he had.

Vera watched the exchange between her son and her angel as she was coming to think of Eliza. She had a knowing look on her face.

"Let's set the table," Vera interrupted Eliza's thoughts. It would do her no good wanting something she could never have. She quickly set the table telling Vera to sit and relax.

This time, Vera did as told. "Could you get me a glass of 7 Up?"

Eliza's concern appeared immediately. "It's not your stomach bothering you, is it?"

"Oh, no dear. I'm just thirsty. That's all. I can't wait to dig into a dish of those chicken and peppers. It's been a long time that I've been able to enjoy good food."

Minutes later, Jason returned with Angel. She ran to her grandmother and gave her a kiss. "Grandma, you won't believe what I've learned. I've learned how to spell apple. A-P-P-L-E."

"That's marvelous, my precious child. I always said you were like your Daddy. Smart as a whip."

Angel beamed at the compliment; then turned her attention to Eliza. "Oh, Eliza, that smells heavenly. My tummy is rumbling just like Winnie the Pooh's."

"Sit then, and I'll serve you first," Eliza had no problem serving people. The cooking? Something she couldn't get the hang of though she did make an excellent Italian sub that afternoon.

As if reading her thoughts, Jason said, "That sub was delicious. You could spoil a man whipping up things like that in the middle of the day."

"You just wait and see what our Eliza will be making for lunches. I'm going to give her some of my other recipes," Vera intervened.

"I'll be sure to put on ten pounds."

Once Eliza had served everybody, she sat down with a plate of her own. When she tasted the food on her plate, she almost moaned aloud. Truly scrumptious.

"No dessert tonight," Vera said, "but tomorrow I'm going to give Eliza my recipe for strawberry cheesecake."

"Yum," Angel said.

Her father seconded the opinion.

As they had the previous night, both father and daughter cleared their plates and placed them in the dishwasher.

"Well, I'm going back up to the office to make a few calls on some bids, but I should be done early. Do you mind if I join you and Angel during playtime tonight?"

Eliza's hand fluttered up to her throat and she grabbed onto her pearl necklace. "Oh my, no not at all. In fact, we'd love the company. Wouldn't we Angel?"

"Yeah, Daddy! You can play Chutes and Ladders with us."

"It's a deal, but I'd better get going on those calls. See you all in a bit. Mother, do you need some help upstairs?"

"No, actually I'm feeling quite good and would like to watch the three of you play for a little while."

Jason backtracked and kissed his mother's cheek. "Fine. I'm so glad to see you feeling more alive. Maybe you can lick this thing after all," Jason walked away whistling.

Vera turned to Eliza aware that Angel was hanging on to their every word. "He's not accepting it, yet."

"But grandma, maybe you're getting better," she impulsively threw her arms around Vera, "I don't want you to go and leave us."

"My darling Angel, sometimes when you're time is up it's up. When God wants me, He'll come for me, and until then I plan on playing lots of games with you."

Eliza poured Vera a cup of coffee. "Angel, do you want to go to your room and read while I clean up? I'll come for you when I'm done."

"Sure Eliza," Angel skipped off as though she hadn't a care in the world. Eliza felt the strong sense of hope emanating from both father and daughter.

Vera was the first to speak. "If I didn't know better, I'd actually believe I have a long time to live. I do know better though, and my doctor will confirm it tomorrow morning. I have to go for some tests to see if the cancer has spread."

"Still, you may live a lot longer than if you stayed on that dreadful chemotherapy."

Vera patted Eliza's hand. "You're as hopeful as my son and granddaughter. God bless you for coming into our lives. Now, I don't mean to insult you. You made the coffee just right, but for some reason I can't drink it. It makes me queasy. How about another glass of 7 Up."

"Here you go," Eliza said as she planted the glass in front of Vera. She then proceeded to clear away the dishes and wipe down the counters. Twenty minutes later Eliza sank into one of the chairs. "Whew! I'm feeling a bit winded."

"You could retire early and let Jason and Angel play alone," Vera offered.

"Oh no no no. I'm not tired, yet, and I promised I'd play the harp for Angel tonight."

Vera looked thoughtful. "Would you mind doing me a favor, Eliza?"

"Of course not. What do you need?"

"When you're out Christmas shopping would you pick up a few things on my list for Jason and Angel?"

"Absolutely. I can't believe it's only four weeks until Christmas," then the thought hit her. She voiced her question aloud. "How on earth am I going to cook Christmas dinner and a special breakfast in the morning?"

Vera chuckled. "You leave it to me. We'll have turkey and stuffing... the works, and for breakfast, I've always made strawberry crepes with whipped cream."

"Vera you better not go off and die on me before then," she wagged her finger at the older woman, "because I'll come looking for you. Turkey dinner with all the fixings. Now that's one for Glory to hear."

Vera immediately perked up. "Who is Glory, if I'm not being too nosey?"

Eliza realized she'd better be careful here or Vera would be inviting her over for dinner every night because she thought Eliza had no one in this world that cared about her. "Oh, she's an old friend from school, but she lives out of town."

"Too bad. It would be nice for you to have a friend close by. You always have us though should you ever need anything. Is my son taking care of your benefits?"

"Yes, and he's giving me a wonderful salary," Eliza quickly added, "And room and board."

"Good because believe you me, you can't afford to be without your benefits today."

Eliza smiled. Vera sounded like a grandmother.

CHAPTER SEVEN

A short while later Jason, Eliza and Angel sat on the floor beneath the Christmas tree playing Chutes and Ladders while a tired Vera looked on. In the end, Angel won the game and Eliza lost.

"What do you think, Eliza? We've been beaten by a six-year-old."

"She's an awfully sharp one, too. Wait until she grows up, Daddy, you're going to have your hands full."

Angel giggled.

Eliza looked up at the Christmas tree. "It's the grandest tree I've ever seen," she whispered.

"It is something, isn't it? Kathleen worked so hard over the years collecting angels. She believed in them, too," Jason looked wistful. He looked at Eliza for a long time, "You're as pretty as one of those angels and act like one."

Eliza blushed. She hoped no one could tell because the only lights in the room twinkled on and off. She started feeling it. Slowly, ever so slowly she felt Jason's growing affection for her. *Okay Buddy Upstairs, you'd better tell me why I'm feeling this way when I'm not supposed to.* He had the softest brown eyes she'd ever seen—even more beautiful than Glory's, and they spoke to her. They told her he found her attractive. He didn't need to tell her he thought her pretty. She already sensed he felt she felt that. His medium brown hair just about matched his eyes, but his heart had become her ultimate weakness. The man cared deeply for those he loved and took good care of them. Though they really hadn't been alone, except for the day in his office, she felt as though she knew him. *That* made her nervous.

"Thank you for the compliment," she mustered up. Vera sat off on the sidelines taking it all in. If a stranger came into the house and watched them play, they'd think them a family. Vera said her prayers to God. She'd love nothing better than to know that Jason and Angel would be well taken care of when she was gone. With Eliza she knew they would, and she knew by their actions they were attracted to each other. She finally felt weak and knew she had to go upstairs, so she addressed her son.

"Jason, would you mind walking me back to my room? I'm feeling a bit tired."

Eliza jumped in. "I could take you," she looked at Jason, "Then, I could help her put on her nightclothes."

"Sure. Would that be all right with you, Mom?"

"Certainly, but give an old lady a boost would you now."

Jason gently lifted his mother from the chair and steadied her. Once he felt she was strong enough, he handed her over to a waiting Eliza.

Eliza quickly put her arm around Vera. Slowly, they made their way back up the stairs.

"You know, you and Jason make quite the family," Vera said. She continued, "I do believe he's taken a fancy to you, and believe me that's a miracle. He hasn't even looked at another woman since Kathleen passed on, and here, tonight, he's telling you you're pretty."

The conversation made Eliza nervous. She didn't know how to reply because she didn't want to insult her by saying she wasn't interested in her son—especially when she really did find her son more than attractive. "Vera, now you quit playing matchmaker and let nature take its course."

"That's me. A meddlesome old woman ready to move on. I don't think I'll go not knowing there'll be someone to take care of him and Angel."

61

"Well, according to your son, I'll be Angel's permanent nanny. I promise to take extra good care of them."

"But, you need someone to love. I feel it Eliza," they reached the top of the stairs. Eliza felt confused. Usually, she had the *feelings*, she said a quick prayer to God to give her the strength to complete this mission successfully while she guided Vera into her room.

"Let me help you with your dress," Eliza unzipped it and it fell to the floor. Eliza shuddered when she looked at how frail Vera looked. The chemo had taken its toll. Her bones just stuck through her skin. She quickly slipped a nightgown over her head and then unsnapped her bra. Since Vera wasn't going anywhere she hadn't bothered with panty hose. One less thing for Eliza to worry about. "Your panties. Do you sleep with them on?"

"I'm the old-fashioned sort, Eliza. So the answer to that would be yes."

"Good. Now, let's slide you into that bed. It sure does look comfortable."

Vera managed to get into a comfortable position, and Eliza adjusted her covers. "What's for breakfast tomorrow morning? Cooking Queen."

Vera smiled a secret smile. "French toast like you've never tasted before. Wake me at six before Jason and Angel go downstairs."

"You've got it. Goodnight now, and have a peaceful sleep," she gently picked up Vera's hand and kissed it. She walked out of the room and back into the living room. No sign of Jason and Angel. They'd stashed the game neatly among the other toys. She assumed Jason took over the roll of reading a bedtime story to Angel.

"It is beautiful, isn't it?"

Eliza jumped. She hadn't sensed Jason's presence until just that moment. Something... her perceptions... She'd better get in touch with Glory.

"One of the nicest I've ever seen. Where on earth did you get that tree?"

"A tree farm not too far from here. We always put up the biggest tree we can find. Would you care to go into the kitchen for some coffee? Angel's sound asleep. I'll even make it," Jason winked.

"Yes, well, I now know how to grind beans, thank you."

"I'm just teasing, Eliza. I'm also sorry we didn't get to hear you play your harp tonight."

"They'll be other nights," Eliza assured him.

"Tonight was special. It felt good to be on the floor playing with Angel. My work sometimes takes up so much of my time."

"Well, you've got a business to run, and Angel understands. What is it they say? Better to have quality time than quantity time?"

"I hired an old friend of mine, Jeff Watkins, to help out. This way, I'll have more time to spend with Angel, especially on the weekends. I'd like to take her to the movies and for ice cream and just for long drives. Maybe even horseback riding."

That got Eliza's full attention. "You ride horses?"

"I haven't in a long time. Kathleen and I used to go every weekend before we had Angel and before my business took me away."

Eliza sensed guilt. Good. Not that he was feeling guilty. That she sensed feelings again. "Life's funny. We all have our paths."

"But, sometimes it's hard to figure which one to take," Jason rubbed his five o'clock shadow. It made him look even more appealing, Eliza couldn't help but think.

"I'd like it if you'd join us," he looked Eliza straight in the eye. She felt it now strong. Her little prayer must have helped. He had powerful feelings for her that she had yet to define.

"I wouldn't want to get in the way of you and Angel..."

"You wouldn't. Angel adores you. That's all she talks about on the way to school. Silly me." Jason slapped his forehead, "Here I am thinking about us when you probably want to spend your free time with your boyfriend. What's his name?"

The moment of truth had approached. Would the angel, Eliza, lie?

"I don't have one at the moment," she said quietly. Truth won out.

"I see. Maybe you'd enjoy joining us sometime?"

"That sounds lovely."

Jason couldn't help himself. He grabbed Eliza's left hand, "No engagement ring."

"No. No engagement ring," she felt it again. A powerful feeling of something kind and caring and something else she couldn't define. She gently pulled her hand from his. "I'll be retiring to my room now, so I'll pass on the coffee. I'll have breakfast at seven."

"Thank you, Eliza. For everything," Jason turned and walked in the direction of his room.

Eliza scooted up the steps and into the safety of her room. She quickly changed while debating if she should call Glory. Rats. She had to come clean. Maybe it would put her feelings in perspective. She picked up her cell phone.

"I've been waiting for this phone call," Glory said.

"Glory, I can't help it. He's so considerate and kind not to mention devastatingly handsome."

"He's still off limits, Eliza. You're to be the bridge for Vera and her family, and then find Jason a wife. That's the assignment as far as I'm told."

"I know which is why I'm telling you. I needed to get this out of my system. I never expected to meet a man like Jason Abbott. I've never felt such powerful feelings before directed at me."

"What kind of feelings?"

"That I don't know. Not yet, anyway, but they're good feelings, and they make me feel… oh, I can't explain it. I'll be a good angel. By the way, the cooking is coming along fine. Vera's doing all of it and letting me take credit."

Glory laughed. "We'll still get you into angel cooking school yet. Goodnight Eliza, and pray on it. God knows what's best."

"Goodnight," Eliza slowly returned her cell phone to her purse. She looked in the mirror wondering what Jason saw. She had long blonde hair like his daughter's. Big blue eyes. A tiny nose. A nice smile. She knew many considered her beautiful, but all she could see was body parts. She didn't know how to put the whole package together.

As she looked at herself she started to wonder what Kathleen looked like. She didn't see any pictures of her around the house–at least not in the rooms she'd been in. She'd have to ask Angel to show her a picture of her Mommy. Eliza slipped into her satin jammies and pulled back the covers. Tomorrow was another day. Her head barely hit the pillow before she fell into a deep, restful sleep.

The alarm went off promptly at five thirty, and Eliza promptly and quickly took a shower and dressed. She picked a soft pink angora sweater and ivory skirt. She knew she dressed up a bit, but she didn't need to do any housework today. That would come tomorrow, so good thing she brought sweats. At six o'clock she tapped on Vera's door. Vera surprised her when she opened it and appeared fully dressed.

"I'm ready to let you watch me whip up the best batch of French Toast this side of the—well, whatever. Jason and Angel love it, and you will, too."

"I'm sure I will. When are you going to actually let me cook?"

Vera smiled her gentle smile. "When I'm too sick to do it anymore. So pay attention to what I'm doing."

"You've got it, Chief," Speaking of Chief, Eliza realized she hadn't talked to the *Big Guy last night* like she planned. Then again, the whole night turned out differently than she expected.

Eliza escorted Vera down the stairs and into the fully equipped kitchen. Vera immediately dug into the bread box. "I make my French toast with sourdough bread. Nice big chunks of it," she said as she cut the bread into large pieces. She dug into the cabinets and came up with a big stainless steel bowl. "Now here's the secret ingredient. Cinnamon. You take a couple eggs, some milk and lots of cinnamon," she talked as she worked. "Then you butter the pan real good. Dip the bread into the mix and let it fry until it's brown on both sides. That's it," she continued turning the bread back and forth. "Now it's your turn. Flip the bread one more time; then put them on the plates."

Eliza followed her instructions.

"Now let's sift a little powdered sugar on these babies, and whala! You've got another delicious, but easy recipe."

"Well we finished in the nick of time. Here come the troops."

"Good morning, Mom," Jason kissed his mother's cheek. "Eliza," he addressed her in a way that made her feel like more than just a housekeeper and nanny. "What have we here? Angel, you're going to love this morning's breakfast."

Angel peeked her head through her father's arm. "Ooooh! French toast. My favorite."

"Well, let's not stand around gawking. Sit down and eat!" Vera shooed them into their seats, then took her own. She watched as Eliza carefully distributed the food. A little while and quite a few pieces of French toast later the group broke up.

"Eliza," Angel spoke up, "Do you think we can play the harp tonight instead of dolls or games?"

"Sure Sweetie."

"Would you mind if I sat in and watched you play, too?" Vera asked.

"That would be fine."

"Never one to be left out. Would you mind an audience of three?" Jason probed.

Eliza actually laughed. He sounded so unsure of himself, but she knew he really wanted to be with her tonight. She felt it. She also wanted to catch him alone so they could discuss Angel's problem with sleeping in her own room. She felt Angel was ready to take the plunge.

"Mom, I didn't forget about your doctor's appointment. It's at ten, right?"

Vera nodded. She dreaded going to see Dr. Ames. She knew, in her heart, the cancer had spread despite the fact she felt so much better. Coming off chemo though made her able to not use hospice and to live life again. He strongly disagreed with her decision. She knew that, but she didn't care. She knew what was right for her and her family.

Eliza saw an opportunity there. "Jason, while the two of you are gone would you mind if I went out and did a little Christmas shopping?"

"Of course not. Take all the time you need," Jason grabbed

Angel's hand, "and you look quite pretty today."

"I dressed all by myself this morning," a happy Angel bragged.

"Oh dear, I forgot to dress her. That won't happen again," Eliza said quickly.

Jason intervened. "Actually, I think it's a good thing for her to learn. Let's go, Pumpkin."

Eliza picked out Vera's prettiest dress and boots. After helping her into them, she proceeded to do her hair. "You know, you have beautiful hair."

"Yes, well that's the one thing I didn't loose during my chemotherapy. I'm a mite vain and prayed to God that I might keep it. I believe he answered my prayer. Even the doctor doesn't know why I didn't loose any because my course of treatment was so strong."

"I believe your right, Vera. God was listening. Well, I think you're all ready. Let me run upstairs and get Jason," Eliza turned to leave when Vera stopped her.

"You said you'd pick up a few Christmas presents for me. Do you mind stopping by The Guild Studios. They sell everything from books to statues. I want to give Angel a prayer card and statue of St. Theresa the Little Flower. I want her to grow up knowing God does answer prayers, and he works through other people and saints. You know when St. Theresa answers your prayer, she sends you a rose as a sign. I also have this," Vera handed Eliza a piece of paper with shakey handwriting on it. When she finished reading it, she just looked up at Vera and let the tears stream down her face.

"What do you want me to do with this?" Eliza was puzzled.

"They have a gentleman that works there that does calligraphy. I want him to write this out on parchment and frame it."

"It's beautiful and so sad. Jason's going to treasure it, I'm sure."

"Here's some money. Wipe those tears, and let's get going. I dread these appointments."

Eliza and Vera made their way down the stairs. As they walked, Eliza said, "Vera, why don't we put your bed down on the first floor?"

"Because I can still manage the stairs with a little help. I want to keep strong and get a little exercise."

"Oh," that was all Eliza had to say on the subject. They went into the foyer where Eliza got Vera's winter coat, scarf, hat and gloves. She helped her bundle up. Just as they were finishing, Jason came down the stairs.

"I was just coming to get you, that's perfect timing," Eliza looked at her watch. It read twenty of ten, "Thank goodness the roads are clear this morning."

"Yes," Jason said. He looked different. He looked like a very concerned and worried man. "Come on, Mom. We've got an appointment to keep," he looked at Eliza, and she felt it again—a surge of warmth, "Please take your time shopping. I don't know how long we'll be."

"Thank you. I'll be back in time to pick up Angel and make dinner."

Eliza watched mother and son walk slowly to his black BMW. She then gathered up her coat, hat and purse, slipped on her gloves and walked out the door before she realized she forgot Vera's note. She let herself back in and ran up the stairs. When she got there, she read it over again.

My dearest son,

I'll always watch out for you from the other side. When you feel the sunshine think of me and know that I am happy with others I have loved and who have also passed on. One day we'll meet again. Love transcends time and space. I'll always love you as I know you will me. Be happy and live your life to the fullest for each day is a special gift. Pray for me as I will for you. Until we meet again, my son, my greatest gift from God.

Mom.

Eliza folded the paper and slipped it into her purse. She felt her eyes welling up again. Her job? Not easy even though she knew for certain about the other side. The separation people experienced now that bothered her. She wondered why you had to be separated from those you love. Like her parents. Why couldn't she see them? Yes, she was questioning God. *Hi, Chief. I'm trying real hard, but I have feelings for him, and I know he has strong, powerful feelings for me. I don't know why. You didn't give me the gift of knowing why. You gave me the gift of reading other people's feelings and needs. Just know I'll try. Amen,"* Eliza walked down the stairs as though in a trance. She opened the front door and let herself out into the bitter cold. She wrapped her scarf around her mouth and proceeded to her car. She planned on having fun shopping for Vera, Jason and Angel. She wanted to put death and separation out of her mind.

CHAPTER EIGHT

Eliza pulled her Honda into the parking garage. She placed her ticket on the dashboard so she wouldn't loose it and then have to pay ten dollars. Her first stop would be the men's department store. She wanted to get Jason something traditional and appropriate. Something special, but not something unprofessional and definitely not too expensive. A holiday tie came to mind. As she made her way through the mall, she had to smile. The holiday season had arrived. Moms pushed their babies in strollers. Men in their business suits shopped for their girlfriends or families. Women walked by with bags piled high. All in all, she concluded the day a huge success for retailers. Eliza loved the hustle and bustle of the holidays, and she especially loved the sound of the Salvation Army's bell. To her, it sounded like Christmas right around the corner. She spied Men's LTD. A good place to start. She wove her way through suit coats and dress shirts and trousers and socks, but nothing jumped out at her. She decided to get Angel's present first. She knew exactly what she wanted and where to look. The question in her mind revolved around price. She stepped into the posh jewelry store and a young woman dressed very chic approached her.

"May I help you?" she inquired.

"Yes, as a matter of fact you can because I know exactly what I want."

"We'll see if we have it. If we don't we might be able to order it."

"Wonderful. I'm looking for a necklace for a little girl with a guardian angel on it."

The woman screwed up her face.

"You don't have one?" Eliza looked disappointed.

"No, that's the strange part. We just got a shipment of jewelry in today and it included a little girl's necklace with an angel on it. We planned on shipping it back because we didn't order it."

Eliza was excited. "Can I see it?"

"Certainly. Just let me go in the back and get it," the woman returned immediately with a gold necklace in a black velvet box. Sure enough the guardian angel Eliza imagined dangled from the chain.

"How much is it?" Eliza inquired cautiously. She crossed her fingers hoping it would be in her budget.

"I don't know. I'll have to call the dealer. They didn't include the price on the invoice.

"That's fine. I'll look around while you make the call."

The woman walked away leaving Eliza to look at all the diamond engagement rings. She knew a lot of women would be getting those this Christmas. The woman came back.

"The dealer didn't know for sure, so they said you could have it for twenty-five dollars. That's an incredibly low price for eighteen carat gold, but he insisted it fine."

"I'll take it."

"Would you like it gift wrapped?"

"Yes, please," Eliza watched as the woman wrapped the tiny box in shiny green wrapping paper and topped it with a pretty red bow. She paid for it, and decided the next on the list had to be Vera. As she walked toward the country crafts shop, she spotted a new men's outlet. She darted in and took a quick look around. She didn't find anything of interest in there until she looked at the mannequin. It wore a beautiful sweater in the warmest shade of brown. A brown that reminded her of Jason's hair and eyes. She immediately enlisted the saleslady's help.

"Do you have that sweater in a large by any chance?"

The woman smiled. "I know we only have a few left. Let's check it out and see."

Sure enough they had one left, and it turned out to be half price. She pulled another twenty-five dollars from her purse. Again she had the woman wrap the gift, but not before feeling how soft the sweater was. A quick vision of Jason wearing it and her cuddled up in his arms flashed before her eyes. She had to stop doing this. Next on the list: Vera. She really didn't know what to get her, so she decided to leave the mall and walk down the street to The Guild Studios.

The wind whipped Eliza from head to toe. She snuggled tighter into her black coat with the black fur collar. She also wrapped her scarf higher up on her face. Finally, she arrived at her destination. This store too, happened to be very busy. As she looked around she became fascinated by all the items for sale. She decided she'd better see the gentleman about the calligraphy first. She went to the cash register to inquire.

"He's in the back, dear. Just walk back and tell him Irene sent you. His name is Hank."

Eliza quickly made her way to the back of the store. Only one man sat on a chair, writing. She assumed him to be Hank.

"Excuse me. I'm looking for Hank. Irene sent me back."

The old man smiled. "You've found him. Now, what can I do for you?"

"I'm looking to have this poem done in calligraphy and framed. Do you think you can do it?"

"Sure can. As a matter of fact, I can have it done in an hour. Would that be satisfactory?"

"Yes, that would be fine. I'll leave this with you then. It's the only copy I've got," she said as she handed him Vera's note.

"Not to worry. It's in good hands."

"Thank you," Eliza made her way back into the store. As she walked, she stopped to look at the greeting cards when she spied it. A book titled *A Cook Book for the Soul.* She leafed through it and found herself stunned to find all sorts of delicious sounding recipes each with a spiritual story on the side. She knew God guided her to this very spot. She picked up the book satisfied with Vera's soon-to-be Christmas present. She then made her way through a crowded area to reach the statues. Right away, she saw a beautiful statue of St. Theresa. Large and colorful. That's how she would describe it. She picked up the statue and looked underneath for the price. It was fifty dollars. She didn't know how much Vera wanted to spend, but decided to buy it anyway. She'd kick in a few dollars if Vera needed it. She then went in search of prayer cards. Even as an angel, she never realized how many saints one could pray to. Finally, she located St. Theresa's prayer card. Only one dollar and fifty cents. Satisfied with her purchases, she went to the counter.

"Ah, she's a beauty," the saleslady said in reference to St. Theresa.

"She is. I'm also having a poem written and framed by Hank. Can I pay for it now and then come back for it?"

"Certainly. The framed art is thirty-five dollars."

The woman rang up all her purchases including the cookbook.

A couple minutes later Eliza smiled and assured the lady she'd be back in an hour for the frame. She put up her fur collar and battled the wind that bit at her cheeks, the only bare spot on her body. She felt relieved to be back in the mall and dreaded having to go back out in the weather in a little while. She decided to go to the coffee room and have a cup of hot cocoa since she had finished her shopping. She found a table window side towards the back of the room. When the waitress came, she ordered a Danish along with her hot chocolate.

"Extra whipped cream, please," When the waitress walked away, Eliza pulled the cookbook from the bag and started flipping through the pages. The introduction told the recipes had been handed down through the generations as comfort food. One story caught her eye. A recipe for beef stroganoff. It went on to tell how this meal brought together the entire family every Sunday. The story of love and togetherness touched Eliza's heart. She knew Vera would love it. The area in the back of the book left space to write recipes of your own. Eliza thought how wonderful it would be for Vera to write her recipes down and pass the book down to Angel.

Soon the waitress came with Angel's cocoa and Danish. She savored the taste of cheese, pastry and frosting. It hit the spot, and the cocoa warmed her from the inside out. She sat thinking about her purchases. It seemed it had been too easy to find the right presents. She wondered if Glory had anything to do with it. So, she decided to find out. She dug in her purse for her cell phone.

"Glory here, Eliza," the woman's voice was soft and sweet.

"How did you know it was me?" Eliza asked.

"Lucky guess. That, and I haven't heard from you in a while. Oh, and caller ID from down on earth AND above."

"I'm Christmas shopping. You wouldn't by any chance have planted gifts in any of the stores?"

The silence loomed. Glory didn't say anything for quite a while or so it seemed to Eliza. Then she finally answered. "No, Eliza. I didn't," when she heard about Eliza's purchases and how perfect they were...and the story about the necklace, Glory slowly answered.

"It sounds more like God is working in your corner."

"Yes, well things are working out fine."

"You mean with Jason?"

"I have my feelings under control and back in check."

"Good. Where are you now?"

"I'm sitting inside a coffee house having hot chocolate. These temperatures are frigid. I have to go back outside the mall to another store to pick up Vera's present for her son."

"Enjoy your holiday shopping, Eliza. I've got to run," Glory clicked off.

Eliza folded her phone in half and stuck it back in her purse. She looked at her watch. She had been so caught up in the cook book, she didn't even realize the time. She paid her bill, left a generous tip on the table and proceeded back to The Guild. Once inside, she headed to the back to seek out Hank. When she found him, he just smiled at her. "I think you'll like this one," he handed her an eight by ten matted frame. Eliza had to admit she'd never seen anything as beautiful. Not only the handwriting, but in the background the sunshine and a rainbow and fluffy white clouds. And, of course, what the picture read made it all the more important and impressive and sentimental.

"Oh, Hank. It's just perfect. Thank you," she reached up and kissed the man on the cheek. "You don't know what this will mean to someone."

Hank blushed. "I'm an artist and only do the best work I can, God willing."

"Well, you did an extraordinary job on this."

"If you want it wrapped, just take it to the front desk."

"No, I want to show it to someone first. I'll wrap it."

"Well then, here's a bag," Hank slid the frame into a large Guild Studio's bag, "Come again."

Eliza battled the bitter cold once more. By the time she reached the parking garage she realized the time. Almost one. She drove down the ramp and paid her two dollars, and then headed for her new home.

She pulled into her parking spot and Jason's car sat there. Their appointment at the doctor's obviously over. Eliza wondered what she would walk in to find. She opened the door, but didn't see anyone right away. She hung up her things, hid the packages in the back of the closet and made her way to the kitchen. No one there, she backtracked and marched up the stairs. *Dear God*, she prayed, *let Vera be okay*. She knocked on Vera's door. Jason answered.

"Come in Eliza."

Eliza entered the room not knowing what to expect. She knew the woman approached death every day, but she had that part of her that held out hope for a longer life for Vera, at least until Jason and Angel settled with a new wife and mother.

"Come here Dear," Vera commanded gently.

Eliza sat on the side of the bed. "How are we?"

"We are in remission. The cancer hasn't spread, and the doctors have no idea why I'm still alive. I told them God wasn't ready for me, yet."

Eliza hugged Vera. "That's such good news," she turned to Jason and found herself in his arms. He squeezed her tight.

"The best news I've heard in a long time. You're good for Mom. I hope you're happy here and plan to stay with us for a while."

Eliza's sensors went on. She felt Jason's arms around her as strong as she had imagined when buying his sweater. She felt safe in them and something else… something difficult to explain. She made the mistake of looking up. His eyes were on her mouth. She immediately disengaged herself and grabbed Vera's hand. "Then I guess it's okay for you to come down and watch me whip up another one of your recipes," she winked at Vera.

Vera smiled. "I have just the recipe for this evening."

Jason cleared his voice. "I'll be upstairs if either of you need me."

Eliza faced Jason and felt her heart drop to her stomach. He looked so handsome standing there in his camel sweater and trousers. He also looked a few years younger and very relieved. "Thank you for giving me time off to shop. I had a lot of fun today."

"This isn't a prison, Eliza. You're free to come and go as you please, and invite anyone you wish over for visits."

When Jason left, Eliza grabbed Vera's two hands. "Let's go cook."

Once in the kitchen, Vera started barking out orders. "Thaw the beef cubes in the microwave. Get out a can of cream of mushroom soup, sour cream, olive oil and noodles."

"Check, check and double check. I have everything you requested. Now are you going to tell me what we're making?"

"Beef stroganoff." Vera said simply.

Eliza's eyes popped. Was it just mere coincidence. In her line of work, she learned very few things were coincidence.

"Now this is another real easy one. I'm going to sit and supervise today."

"But, what if I ruin it," Eliza said nervously.

"You won't. Trust me, Eliza. You can do this. Now add a good amount of olive oil to the fry pan. Like we did for the chicken and peppers."

Eliza recalled how much oil Vera had used. She poured the oil until it covered the entire bottom of the big fry pan.

"Turn it on high. Once it starts spitting, add the beef cubes."

"Eliza did as told. Soon she dumped in the beef cubes.

"Now, you have to brown them real good until they're nice and tender. Keep stirring them around so that you get all sides."

Eliza found this job easier than she thought. With that finished, Vera instructed her to dump the mushroom soup into the pan along with one can of water.

"Now let that simmer for a good half hour. That means we have time to chat."

Eliza set the stove to simmer and then joined Vera at the table.

"I got your presents. Would you like to see them? I've stashed them in the closet for now."

"Please," Vera said.

Eliza retrieved the bags with the statue, prayer card and framed art. She set them on the table.

Vera just ran her hands up and down the statue. "She's beautiful."

"That's exactly what the saleslady said. And here's the prayer card. Now, for your note." Eliza slowly pulled the frame from the bag. She handed it over to Vera."

Eliza could see Vera's eyes water. "It's perfect."

"I didn't have it wrapped because I knew you'd want to see it first, and I didn't even think to have Angel's present wrapped. I can do that later."

"No, Honey. I'll do it myself. Can you put these in the bottom of my closet upstairs?"

"Sure," Eliza carried the gifts and did as requested, stopping along the way to retrieve her presents so she could slip them in her room. She hurried down the stairs to check on her dinner even though she knew Vera kept a close eye on it. Maybe she could cook after all.

As soon as she entered the kitchen, she could smell the heavenly aroma. She sat across from Vera. "How are you feeling inside right now, Vera?" Eliza sensed the woman had mixed feelings.

"I'm grateful that I might be around to see my son settled down and granddaughter with a mother."

"Have you been praying for that?" Eliza quickly added, "You don't have to answer that if it's too personal."

"No, Eliza, I pray that God takes care of things. I leave everything up to him, but there's nothing I wouldn't love more than to be at my son's second wedding. That's our secret. Jason would flip if he heard me say that."

"You know, I meant to ask Angel this, but I haven't seen any pictures of Kathleen in the house. Why?"

"Jason keeps one on his desk, and Angel has one in her room on her desk. Next time you take her in to change take a look. She was a beautiful woman. Completely opposite of you. She had dark skin and hair, but she was a sweet girl, that Kathleen. She treated my son and Angel—let's just say, she made the perfect daughter-in-law. We got along wonderfully."

"But, you said they were more friends than husband and wife."

"They were. Anyone could see it, but they also were a family. A very close family."

"Oh, you know what? Shouldn't we be making strawberry cheesecake?"

Vera chuckled. "I'll leave the stroganoff to you, and I'll start right on the cheesecake. You can add the container of sour cream to the beef. Stir it good and let it simmer. The longer it simmers, the more tender the meat."

As Eliza followed Vera's instructions, she watched out of the corner of her eye as Vera started whipping up a cheesecake. It amazed her how adept this woman could be in the kitchen. Despite her illness.

When two fifteen rolled around, Eliza asked Vera if she'd keep an eye on her stroganoff. Vera shoed her out of the kitchen. "Go get my Angel Baby."

CHAPTER NINE

Eliza arrived at the school right on time. Bill Wiggins stood in his usual spot. As usual, he tried to strike up a conversation with Eliza. Though a handsome and friendly man, Eliza had no interest. A man with brown eyes and brown hair had captured her heart, and she had to learn to remember she could never, ever have him.

"Eliza, Eliza," Angel bounded toward her, "Look what I made in school today!" she said with all the enthusiasm of a child.

Eliza oohed and ahhed over the multi-colored fan. "Let's go home and show your Grandma and Daddy. I think they'll be proud of you."

As Eliza buckled Angel into her seat, the little girl inquired, "You are going to play the harp for us tonight, aren't you?"

She ruffled the little girl's blonde curls as she'd seen her father do so many times. "If that's what you want."

"Goody! And can I play it, too?"

"Yes, you can," Eliza turned the radio to a classic rock station and started humming along to a song by The Beatles. Home came quicker than she thought. She enjoyed herself with Angel and their private moments.

Angel dashed for the door. She ran straight upstairs to the third floor with her fan. Meanwhile, Eliza checked in on Vera in the kitchen. She just sat at the kitchen table staring off into space.

"Hello," Eliza waved her hand in front of Vera's face.

"Oh, Eliza, your back already. I turned off the stroganoff. It's finished. All we have to do is reheat it at dinner time. Cheesecake's in the oven. When my Henry died, I didn't think I could go on living. Somehow I managed as Jason has, but I always knew in my heart, Henry was my soul mate. Kathleen wasn't Jason's soul mate, no matter how close they were."

Eliza wondered why the sudden turn in conversation.

"I'm telling you this because I think there is something strong between you and my son."

Eliza shushed Vera, "I warned you about playing matchmaker."

"I know, but when you don't know how much time you have left you tend to say what's on your mind. I hope you'll at least consider a relationship with my son should he pursue you."

Eliza didn't know how to answer, so she said the best thing that she could. "We'll see if he ever pursues me."

"A mother knows things, Eliza. You'd better go after Angel and help her get changed. Everything in the kitchen is under control."

Eliza headed directly for Angel's room. When she knocked on the door, Angel didn't answer. She quietly said the little girl's name. Still no answer. She knew Angel must be up on the third floor with her father. She didn't want to interrupt them, but something pushed her up the stairs. Once she reached Jason's office she overheard Angel.

"She doesn't look like Mommy, but she's real pretty and nice."

"I know, Sweetie."

"Maybe she could be my step Mommy."

For the tenth time, Jason had to answer his daughter. "I told you before Angel, it's not that easy. Honey, she's your nanny—and a good nanny. She really cares about you and grandma. I can see that. Okay?"

"Okay," Angel sounded dejected.

Once again, Eliza felt like she eavesdropped. The door opened, and she stood there not knowing what to say. Caught in the act.

"Eliza, what can I do for you?" instead of sounding disturbed, he sounded happy to see her.

"Actually, I'm looking for Angel. I wanted to help her undress. I also wanted to schedule a time when I could talk to you in private."

"Angel," Jason looked at his daughter, "Do you think you could get changed by yourself?"

Angel nodded her head.

"Angel, when you're done, you can visit with your grandmother. She's in the kitchen," Eliza added.

Angel left and, once again, Eliza sensed Jason's feelings strong and clear. She sensed his embarrassment. He knew she'd overheard their conversation. She immediately wanted to put him at ease. "Children have vivid imaginations, don't they?"

"You can say that again," Jason laughed, "Angel has some crazy notion about you being her step Mommy. I'm sorry if that makes you uncomfortable."

"It doesn't. I know she's little and doesn't understand relationships, yet."

Jason veered the conversation away from Angel and her fantasies. "You said you wanted to see me?"

"It's about Angel's sleeping arrangement. I wondered when you thought she could try sleeping in her own room. I'm just down the hall, and I could even stay with her until she falls asleep."

Jason rubbed his chin. "I know she should sleep on her own. She told me she has bad dreams, but she won't tell me what they're about."

Eliza decided to tell Jason part of it. Angel hadn't sworn her to secrecy.

"She dreams that the devil takes your wife from heaven."

Jason looked surprised that Angel had confided in Eliza and not him.

"I think it best you don't mention anything to her until she's ready to tell you. Maybe you could talk about monsters and such to get her to open up."

"I will. Why don't we approach Angel after dinner tonight? See how she feels about moving back into her room? And I can read to her until she's asleep."

"I think that's a positive step in the right direction, and I'll be just down the hall if she needs me in the middle of the night."

Jason got up from his desk and walked around it until he was face to face with Eliza. He reached for her hand and, once again, Eliza felt it. It was like a sudden whoosh of warmth, this time with tingling throughout her whole body.

"I can't thank you enough for what you've done so far for my family. They mean everything to me."

Eliza allowed him to continue to hold her hand, but still had overwhelming sensations. "Me, too. There's beef stroganoff and cheesecake for dinner tonight. If you'd like to eat early, it's ready."

"That sounds like a good idea. I'll be down in a few minutes."

This time, Eliza didn't bump into the door, but she couldn't shake the feelings Jason left her with. She didn't know which feelings were hers or his. Something like this never happened to her, and it frightened her. She made it to the kitchen in record time. Vera barely greeted her, engrossed in reading a book to Angel. She didn't disturb them. Instead, she quickly turned on the burner where the stroganoff sat, and just as quickly and efficiently set the table. Just as she finished Jason walked in. The first thing he did? Kiss his mother. "I hear we're having another one of your famous recipes tonight."

"Eliza's doing just fine with my recipes. Aren't you, Child?"

Eliza turned a shade of pink. Lying? Not her forte, but she had made half of the night's meal. "I'm trying," She could say that truthfully.

As they ate, Eliza just listened to the conversation between generations. It reminded her of something she read in the cookbook she'd bought for Vera. Jason first noticed her silence.

"You're quiet tonight, Eliza. Are you feeling okay?"

"Just a little tuckered out from my Christmas shopping. The mall seemed exceptionally crazy today."

Angel's ears perked up. "You went Christmas shopping?" without waiting for an answer she asked Eliza, "Could you take me Christmas shopping for Daddy and grandma's presents."

Eliza responded. "If it's okay with your father, then yes."

"Daddy, can she?"

Jason smiled at Eliza from across the table. "She sure can."

"That's great, but you're going to have to open my piggy bank for me."

"I will when you and Eliza figure out when you're going to go shopping."

"Angel," Eliza addressed the excited little girl, "we can go some afternoon right after school. How does that sound?"

"When Eliza?" the little girl persisted.

"How about next week. I've got some housekeeping to tend to here. I've been so focused on cooking that I really haven't done more than dust and mop the floors."

"I'll help you, Eliza," Angel volunteered.

"What a wonderful offer. I'll take you up on that."

"Then maybe we'll get done quicker and can go shopping sooner."

Eliza had to laugh at how the little girl's mind worked. "We'll see how things go. No promises, okay?"

"Okay," she sounded as dejected as she had only an hour ago in her father's office.

"I think we're in for a recital this evening," Vera cut through the silence. Immediately, Angel's eyes lit up.

"And I'm going to get to play, right?"

"Absolutely. So why don't you let me clean up."

"I can bring the harp down and put it in the living room," Jason offered.

Eliza looked into his eyes and knew he cared. "That would be lovely."

Angel and her father left the kitchen hand in hand. Vera just sat and watched as Eliza cleaned up the mess.

"You have no problem with housekeeping skills. I'll give you that," the older woman teased.

"Yes, well it's pretty basic isn't it?"

"Where did you learn to play the harp?"

"I taught myself. Like I told Jason. It's an intuitive thing."

Vera nodded. "Nothing like a woman's intuition. I've always been told I have a good one."

Eliza knew exactly where she planned on taking this conversation and put a stop to it. "Then maybe you'd be great at playing the harp."

Vera took the hint and let the subject drop.

"By the way, hospice called to inquire as to how you are. They are thrilled to hear the good news."

"The staff was extremely nice, but not as nice as you."

Eliza smiled at the compliment. "Compliment taken. Thank you. Now let's head into the living room," she wrapped her arm through Vera's and they strolled into the room with the huge Christmas tree. Darkness enveloped them except for the twinkling lights. Eliza immediately spotted her harp in the middle of the room, a chair behind it. Jason and Angel sat on the couch. Jason stood and helped his mother sit down. Eliza went directly to the chair and began plucking away. A half an hour later, Eliza stopped. Everyone applauded. Again, Eliza felt herself blushing. She sensed Jason's admiration. "Come here, Angel. I'll teach you a few things."

Angel hopped right up, eager as could be.

"Now sit down," when Angel sat, Eliza positioned Angel's hands, "Now just pluck any of the strings you want. Just feel the music."

Angel plucked away, smiling the entire time. When she stopped everyone applauded. Angel stood and took a bow.

"That's all for tonight, Angel. That's just to get you used to the strings and the plucking."

"Thank you, Eliza," Angel jumped into her father's lap, "Can we play a game?"

Jason looked at Eliza. "Are you up to being beaten by a six-year-old again?"

Eliza smiled. "Sure, why not. What game, Angel?"

"Mousetrap."

Jason moaned. "You mean the one where I have to put it all together."

"Yep, Daddy."

Once again, the three of them were seated on the floor beneath the Christmas tree while Vera watched the whole scene unfold. Jason and Eliza laughed because they were losing. Angel clapped her hands with glee. A while later, Jason called a halt to the game. "Angel it's time for bed," he decided to broach the subject, "How would you like to sleep in your room tonight? I'll read you a story and stay with you until you fall asleep."

Angel eyes darted to Eliza. A look of fear crossed her face. Eliza tuned into Angel's feelings. She sensed the confusion and fear. Eliza decided to intervene.

"And if you wake in the night, I'll be right down the hall."

Angel hesitated. "Daddy, if I get scared in the night can I come downstairs and sleep with you?"

"Yes, or you can sleep with Eliza."

Angel thought for a minute. "Okay," she turned to Eliza, "I'm ready for my bath now."

"I'll run upstairs and get your stuff. Meet you in the bathroom."

Eliza hurried up the stairs and into Angel's room. She turned on the light and looked for Angel's desk. There it sat. A picture of Kathleen. It shocked Eliza. She expected beautiful... but this? Kathleen made incredibly beautiful, something every woman should strive for every day. The part that confused her? Angel didn't look a thing like her. Where Angel was light and blonde, Kathleen had a dark almost an exotic look. Because Angel didn't look like either of her parents, she actually found herself wondering if Angel could have been adopted, but she knew that couldn't be true because Angel had told her the story of how her mother, after seeing her when born, said she looked like an angel and that's how she got her name. Eliza returned the picture to the desk and gathered up Angel's jammies, underwear and comb and brush. When she reached the bathroom, she found the tub already filled. "Bubble bath tonight?" Eliza asked Angel.

"Daddy said it was okay."

"I leave everything else to you, Eliza, and I'll take Mom upstairs. She assured me she could get changed by herself tonight," Jason squeezed Eliza's elbow as he walked out the door, closing it behind him. The powerful feelings of warmth she'd felt all night got even stronger. Eliza just said a quick prayer and sent it up to The Chief.

Eliza helped Angel undress and into the tub. She suddenly felt overcome by waves of sadness. She also felt Angel's fear. She decided to question her on her feelings. "Angel, honey, are you scared to sleep in your room tonight?"

"What if Daddy cries because I'm not there?"

Eliza thought about that. "Well, I'm sure he'd come get you if he needed you."

"Do you really think so?" the little girl's eyes opened wide. She looked so young and innocent.

"Absolutely. How about your dreams?"

"I can sleep with you if I get scared in the night?"

"Angel, I'm right down the hall. You can climb into my bed, and we'll cuddle, but you might not have those bad dreams anymore. Remember how we talked about there is no such thing as the devil?"

Angel nodded. "I'll sleep in my room tonight if you think that's best."

"Well, you are a big girl now. Besides, you'll be close to your grandmother, too."

For the rest of the bath, Angel was quiet. Eliza sensed her unease, but knew it better for her to start sleeping on her own. She toweled Angel dry, slipped her flannel nightgown over her head and held out her slippers. "Take these, it's a bit drafty," Angel obeyed. "Come on, let's go get your Dad."

Angel hooked onto Eliza's hand and followed her into the living room. Jason sat in the recliner staring up at the tree. When he saw Angel he said, "Come here, Angel Baby," he patted his knees. Angel immediately hopped onto his lap. She threw her arms around his neck, "It'll be okay, Angel. You'll see. Let's go read a bedtime story."

"I'll be in my room Angel, in case you need me."

Angel just looked at Eliza with big, watery eyes.

Eliza bent down and kissed the little one on the cheek. "Remember I told you we were going to chase away those bad dreams with prayers?"

Angel nodded.

"All you have to do is to ask your guardian angel to keep you safe. Dream about snowmen and Santa Claus," she then walked away. Once she reached the top of the stairs, she knocked on Vera's door, but the sickly older woman didn't answer. Eliza peeked in and saw that she slept soundly. She looked better day by day. She walked across the hall to her room and closed the door. She then proceeded to strip down and put on her pajamas. She crawled beneath the covers and sighed. Tomorrow meant another day.

CHAPTER TEN

Eliza felt a tugging on her sleeve. She opened her eyes and saw Angel standing there with her Teddy Bear. "Bad dream?" she asked.

"No, Me and Boo Bear just wanted to cuddle with you."

Eliza folded down the covers and patted the empty space near her. Angel crawled into the bed and placed her head on Eliza's pillow. "That better?"

Angel nodded. "I did real good though didn't I?"

"You did terrific. It takes time to get adjusted to new situations, Angel."

Eliza looked at the alarm clock. It read two forty-five a.m. Eliza felt they had a good start. "Do you want me to rub your back and sing to you?"

"What songs do you know?"

"How about 'You Are My Sunshine'?"

"Okay," Angel rolled onto her side so that Eliza could rub her back.

It took about fifteen minutes of rubbing and singing before Eliza's little angel fell fast asleep. Now the only thing she had to worry about? Waking her up in the morning.

Six a.m. came quickly. Eliza woke before the alarm had a chance to go off. She rolled out of bed and looked at her sleeping angel before going to the closet for her clothes. Today, she intended to do some heavy duty housecleaning, so she pulled out a purple sweat suit and sneakers. She quietly made her way down the hall to the second floor bathroom. Once she showered and changed she knocked on Vera's door. Again, no answer. Eliza worried, so she opened the door. Vera seemed content and sound asleep and snoring. Eliza decided they could make do with cereal and toast this morning. No sense in waking Vera. Eliza figured if Vera's body told her she needed to rest – she needed to rest.

When Eliza walked into the kitchen, she met with a surprise. Jason sat at the table drinking coffee and reading the morning newspaper.

"Good morning. I didn't expect to find you here this early."

Jason put the paper down. "I couldn't sleep. I worried all night about Angel."

"Well, she did good. She crawled into bed with me at quarter to three, but she said she didn't have any nightmares. She just wanted to cuddle. So, I rubbed her back and sang her to sleep. I think that's progress. Don't you?"

Jason agreed, "I guess we'll just have to take it one night at a time," he looked at Eliza closely. He noticed the purple sweat suit. She looked beautiful in it, "Going for a run?"

Eliza looked down at her suit. "No, just have some housework to catch up on."

"Eliza, I'm glad we have a few minutes alone because I want to ask you something. After dinner tonight, would you like to take Angel and Vera, if she's up to it, for a ride around town to see the Christmas lights?"

Eliza sensed it again. He had feelings for her that were not platonic, and that warm feeling penetrated whenever they talked. "I think that's a great idea. I'd love to see the lights. Well, I'd better get organized. I thought maybe we'd have a light breakfast today. You know, just some cereal, juice and toast."

"That sounds fine to me," Jason pretended to read the newspaper, but actually he thought about everything that happened in his life. For some reason, he felt Kathleen would approve of Eliza. He still loved Kathleen with his whole heart, but slowly he came to the conclusion that maybe he didn't have to live the rest of his life alone. He wondered how Eliza felt about him. He didn't know how to approach the situation. She dealt with him as an employer, and he valued her very much. He didn't want to destroy that relationship, but he did want to pursue a different kind of relationship. She had his mother and daughter wrapped around her little finger. He'd have to make sure he found more time with them. Now that Jeff assumed some of his duties it would be do-able. The first thing he wanted to do meant including her in all family events. He wanted her to know how he considered her part of the family. For the first time in a long time he didn't feel guilty thinking about having another woman in his life. Maybe Eliza was the answer to his prayers. Since she began working for him, he didn't have a hard time getting to sleep. He looked forward to mornings and dinner, and now he looked forward to after dinner games and harp playing. He'd prayed hard asking God to give him a sign. Some kind of sign that he should look for a wife and mother for Angel. Maybe Eliza's presence was that sign.

Eliza slowly unloaded the dishwasher and put all the dishes and silverware back in its place. She wiped down the refrigerator and stove before setting the table. She grabbed a couple boxes of cereal, poured the juice and had the toast in the toaster all ready to go. She felt a sense of calmness she hadn't ever felt before, and she knew Jason's presence made all the difference. She also could practically read Jason's mind. As his mother had warned, he might pursue her. Now, for sure, Eliza knew he would. *Big Guy Upstairs, why is this happening to me? I feel something for him I can't explain, and I don't want to feel anything. I just want to see my Mom and Dad. Please let Jason find a woman who would make a good wife and mother. Amen.*

Sure enough at seven o'clock Angel joined Jason and Eliza. "I'll go see if your mother is up," Eliza said. This time when she knocked on the door she got an answer. She opened the door and found Vera looking through her closet for a dress.

"I'm sorry I wasn't up to make breakfast this morning. Last night tuckered me out."

"We're just doing the toast and cereal thing this morning. Jason and Angel don't seem to mind."

"We'll have to work on a special dish for dinner then. How does chili sound?"

"Mmm. I haven't had a good dish of chili in a long, long time."

"You'll have to run to the store for me and get some fresh rolls and Monteray Jack cheese. I have everything else we'll need."

"Jason mentioned taking us all for a ride around town tonight to look at the Christmas lights."

"That sounds fabulous. I can't wait. There's this one house on Apple Street that goes all out. There's usually a line up of cars down the street. Everybody wants to see it because it's so spectacular."

"I'm sure Angel will be thrilled."

"Speaking of my granddaughter, how did she do last night?" Vera looked concerned.

"I think everything went okay. She did sneak into my room in the middle of the night, but she said it wasn't because she had any nightmares. Her and Boo Bear just wanted to cuddle. Little by little, she'll adjust."

"You're like a mama to her."

"I'm her nanny, Vera. I'm only doing my job."

"But, you really care about her."

"Of course I do. What I'm trying to say is any good nanny would have done the same."

Vera raised an eyebrow. "You think what you want, and I'll think what I want. Please zip my dress."

A few minutes later, Vera and Eliza joined Jason and Angel at the table. It seemed their world revolved around food.

"Well, I'm going to have a bowl of Cheerios and some wheat toast," Vera announced, "I'm famished."

Jason smiled at his Mom. It felt so good not to have to watch her barely able to move and throwing up all the time.

Once Jason and Angel left and Vera entered back in her room, Eliza decided to tackle the cleaning. She vacuumed, she scrubbed, she dusted. By noon she had the whole first floor done. She decided to leave the second floor for another day. On impulse, she slipped on her winter coat and picked up her coat and keys. She wanted to get those few items Vera needed for the night's dinner.

She pulled into the Super Shopper and grabbed a cart. When she came to the produce aisle, she picked out a nice head of lettuce, some tomatoes, cucumbers, peppers, radishes everything she thought should be in a good salad. Then she darted to the aisle with the salad dressings. She selected two. One meant red wine and vinegar, the other Italian. As she headed for the bread aisle, she bumped into Bill Wiggins.

"Well, hi there, Eliza," Bill smiled. He dressed as usual in a pair of jeans and workboots. "Fancy meeting you here."

"We all have to eat," Eliza returned the smile, "I'm in a bit of a hurry," before she could get away, Bill stopped her.

"Gee, Eliza. I wondered if maybe you wanted to go see a movie this weekend."

Eliza didn't want to hurt the man's feelings, but she didn't want to get involved in the human dating scene. "I'm sorry, Bill, I can't. Maybe some other time."

"Yeah, maybe some other time," he said sounding a little down. "I'll see you at the school later."

Eliza zoomed down the bread aisle and picked up a loaf of crusty French bread. She also got real butter and the cheese. Satisfied she had everything, she went to the check out counter only to discover Bill Wiggins.

"We meet again," he said with no emotion.

Eliza knew his ego had taken a blow, and she wanted to soften it. "You must have lots of women chasing after you, Bill. I'm sure you'll find someone to go to the movies with this weekend."

He didn't say anything. Eliza could feel how rejected he felt. "We'll have to get the kids together to play in the park one day after school once the weather gets nice."

That gave him hope. He smiled. "Sure thing, Eliza," he paid the cashier and went on his way.

Not long after Eliza put away the groceries. Vera delighted in the fact that she could make a big salad. "I even have some shredded mozzarella to sprinkle on top," she said pleased with herself.

Many hours and full stomachs later, the foursome climbed into Jason's SUV and headed out to see the Christmas lights.

"Oh, Daddy, Daddy, look at that big Santa Claus on the roof!"

The four of them commented on the beautiful presentations throughout the neighborhoods. Then, they got in line to see the house on Apple Street.

Jason turned the radio on to the station that played all Christmas songs. The four of them just sat quietly waiting their turn. When it came, Angel squirmed in her seat with excitement. The front of the house featured moving elves at work, a talking Santa Claus and Mrs. Claus. Holiday music played in the background. Along the side of the house all Angel's favorite Christmas characters moved this way and that. Rudolph and Frosty. Even Charlie Brown, and a million different colored tiny lights lit the house. It looked like something out of a storybook.

"Their electric bill must cost a fortune," Vera commented.

"I would say so," Eliza agreed, "I think it's somebody's bath time," Eliza said squeezing Angel's hand. She had sat next to Eliza, glued to her side.

"Aw, do I have to?"

"Only if you don't want to smell young lady," Jason laughed.

As they approached Jason's house, they all commented on how nice their lights looked, too.

"I'd say this house is as nice as any we've seen," Eliza commented.

"Not as nice as the one with Santa's workshop," Angel responded.

"Pooh! Ours is even nicer," at that moment, Jason looked directly into Eliza's heart. She knew he picked up on her saying "ours," she sensed that overwhelming feeling creeping up on her. Sure enough, it hit her again. This time, she sensed a feeling of tenderness coming from Jason. Eliza shook it off and helped Vera into the house.

"Harp tomorrow night," Eliza announced, "Now, let's get this young lady ready for bed. I'm going to scrub you clean like I did the house today."

Angel ran upstairs for her jammies and Boo Bear. Eliza went into the bathroom and filled the tub. Jason stuck his head in. "I had a nice time tonight."

Eliza didn't know what to say. Her tongue actually felt stuck. She looked at this man who could grace the cover of every men's magazine she'd ever seen and completely lost focus. His looks alone didn't do it for Eliza. The sincerity behind his words bowled Eliza over. Finally, she managed to squeak out, "Me, too."

"Maybe Saturday night we could take Angel ice skating."

Ah ha! This is how he meant to pursue her. He knew Vera couldn't ice skate, therefore leaving them alone. She didn't want to say no, but she feared saying yes.

Jason sensed her hesitation. "You do know how to skate, don't you?"

"Actually, yes. The little boy I cared for before I came to work for you liked skating, so I took him all the time."

"Then, it's a date? Saturday night?"

"I'm sure Angel will be thrilled to hear we're taking her skating," she said, avoiding the word 'date.'

In the nick of time, Angel came running up to Jason. "I'm ready for my story," she looked at Eliza, "and my prayers to my guardian angel."

Eliza knelt down and opened her arms wide. Angel crawled right into them. "Mmm. You smell so clean."

"Much better than smelly, Angel, isn't it?" Jason laughed again as he said it.

"Oh, Daddy," Angel kissed Eliza's cheek, "I can come into your room again if I wake up?"

"Absolutely."

"Good night, Eliza," Angel said as she disengaged herself from Eliza's arms.

"Yes, good night, Eliza," Jason added and walked off with Angel attached to his arm.

Once Eliza had the bathroom clean and tidy, she headed for her room. She slipped on her nightgown. Quietly, so as not to disturb Jason and Angel, she made her way to the bathroom to brush her teeth. She looked in the mirror and noted the glow that seemed to emanate from her. She put her hands on her cheeks. Did Jason do that to her? *Oh, Chief. How ever am I going to find him a wife?* She plodded along to her room when she overheard Jason and Angel praying the Angel of God prayer. She smiled. Someone from above indeed watched over them.

The next morning Vera woke Eliza instead of the other way around. The elderly lady knocked on her door. Eliza rolled out of bed, rubbing her eyes. When she opened it, she half expected it to be Angel. Instead, a very bright and alert looking Vera stood smiling in the doorway. "Pancakes this morning. Buttermilk with blueberries."

"Oh dear, is it that time already?"

"Yes my little student. Get dressed. I'll wait for you in my room. There's something I want to show you anyway."

Eliza quickly showered and dressed in jeans and a T-shirt. She didn't have to knock on Vera's door because it sat wide open. "Look," she said pointing to the bed to Angel and Jason's presents. Gift wrapped in gold wrapping paper and beautiful white bows, they made an impressive sight.

"They look beautiful, Vera. You're a talented lady. What other hidden talents do you have?"

"Well, for starters I crochet. Can't knit for peanuts, but I can crochet an afghan in a week. What color do you want? It's your Christmas present from me."

"That's so sweet, Vera. I'd love an afghan. How about white?"

"With an angel in the center," Vera said it as though there was no other way to do it, "Let's get cooking."

Once in her domain, Vera whipped up blueberry buttermilk pancakes that had Eliza watering at the mouth. She flipped them with ease—as though she'd been doing it for years. Eliza wondered just how many years. "Pour the juice, sweetie. I'm just about done."

Jason and Angel walked into the room just as Eliza laid down the first plate stacked high with pancakes. She reached into the cabinet and pulled out blueberry and maple syrup. "I think we have something to celebrate. Don't you think so, Daddy?"

Jason looked perplexed.

"Angel spent the entire night in her own room."

Jason looked at his daughter. "Is that true?" not that he doubted Eliza. He just couldn't believe she could adjust that quickly.

Angel beamed. "Yep. Those guardian angels stay with me and protect me all night long. Right, Eliza?"

"You betcha."

Everyone sat and ate and chatted about the excursion the night before. Jason turned to his mother. "I'm taking Angel and Eliza ice skating on Saturday. Would you like to come and watch?"

Vera immediately looked at Eliza and smiled. "No, I think I'll sit this one out, but thank you for asking."

Eliza knew exactly what Vera had in her mind. Something had to be done about her. In her heart though, she knew, if she had to choose a mother-in-law, Vera would be it. Her son so handsome and caring didn't hurt.

Hours later, after the games and harp playing, Eliza plopped herself down on a kitchen chair and flipped through a magazine. She didn't think sleep would come so easily. She mulled over her feelings for Jason. She didn't know him long, but she didn't have to. She had a gift. She could judge someone's character right away, and their instant connection started the day of her interview. She could give in to her feelings, but then she'd never see her parents again. It didn't seem fair. As she came to an advertisement for a shampoo, she sensed him. She looked up from the magazine. Jason stood in the doorway. She wondered how long he had been standing there. Usually, she picked up on these things instantaneously. However, lately, her senses seemed to be jumbled.

"Mind if I join you?"

"No. I didn't know you read Redbook." Eliza smiled knowing that's not what he meant.

"How about a glass of wine and we go into the living room?"

Everything warned Angel of a dangerous situation, but she agreed anyway. "I'll meet you in there."

She sat on the sofa hoping he would sit by her. Sure enough, he handed her a glass of merlot and sat down a respectable distance from her. Neither said anything for a few minutes. They just sipped their wine, but the silence comforted her instead of feeling awkward. It seemed like they had been doing this every night for years. Jason spoke first.

"I love it in this room, even when the Christmas tree's not here. It's filled with all of Angel's favorite toys and dolls. Whenever I take a client on a tour of the house, I always tell them this room is 'lived in.'"

"I like this room, too. It's cozy and warm."

"Kathleen used to say the exact same thing—despite it's size."

"Does it still hurt?" Eliza broached the subject carefully.

"Time does heal. I know that's a bit clichéd, but it's the truth. I loved her, Eliza. I'll never deny that. For the past three years, I've wrestled with my conscious. I made a promise on her deathbed that there'd never be any other woman in my life. She begged me to find another wife and mother for Angel. Only now, I'm beginning to see why," his eyes pierced hers.

Eliza suddenly felt uncomfortable. She started to feel something more intimate developing between them, "I'm glad you're ready to move on. There are a lot of women who'd feel lucky to have you and Angel and Vera as their family."

Jason took Eliza's glass and put it on the table along side his. He moved closer. Eliza knew exactly what to expect to happen, and nothing in this world could stop it. He kissed her. Gently at first and then more demanding. When Eliza moaned and opened her mouth, he slipped his tongue inside. Her tongue touched his and she thought she felt on fire. He wrapped his arms around her and brought her closer to him. Eliza got lost in sensations she'd never experienced before. Strong and powerful feelings. Jason allowed his need to be right out there in the open daring her to turn him away. She couldn't. She didn't have the strength or desire to let him go. Jason broke the kiss. He put his forehead against hers. "Tell me you wanted that as much as I wanted it."

Eliza's senses started working. Her Mom. Her Dad. All she had at stake, and here she had done the one thing Glory said *The Big Guy Upstairs* didn't want.

"Jason, let's finish our wine."

"I say let's finish our kiss."

"No. It can't happen again, Jason. I'm your employee. I don't want to jeopardize the relationship we already have."

"Are you telling me, you didn't feel it? The power of that kiss?"

Eliza couldn't lie, and she certainly couldn't hurt his feelings. She told him the truth. "I felt it, but that doesn't make it right. Please respect my wishes. I want to be your friend."

Jason sighed. In his heart he knew he'd never give up, not now that he had a taste of Eliza. She belonged to him, and somehow he would see to it that she realized it. He picked up her glass and handed it to her.

"Thank you for respecting my wishes," Eliza's hand shook. Just the brush of his fingertips against hers made her want things she could never have. They sat and finished their wine, neither one saying much.

"I'm going to turn in," Eliza rose. "Thanks for the wine. I think it'll help me sleep," to herself she thought, *now I'll never sleep knowing what it's like to be in your arms kissing you.*

CHAPTER ELEVEN

Friday flew by for Eliza. Vera made her homemade lasagna. Angel had spent another whole night in her room. Everything seemed to be going well. She'd promised Angel that on Monday she'd take her Christmas shopping after school. Only one problem remained. She did something the night before that she had been given strict orders not to do, and she didn't know what to do about it. God knew all, so she had to fess up to Glory. Maybe she could help.

In the privacy of her room, she made the call.

"Glory, I need your guidance. I did it. I got romantically involved with Jason."

Silence filled the air. Finally Glory asked, "Are you continuing this relationship?"

"No. We only shared a kiss, and I told him it couldn't happen again. What should I do? Go through the streets searching for a wife for him?"

"Everything happens for a reason, Eliza. Let it be what it is. A kiss."

"No long lecture on not obeying orders?"

"Eliza, I'm sure you're being hard enough on yourself."

"Did I—I mean can I still see my parents?" she held her breath.

"I'm sure you can as long as you maintain a platonic relationship with Jason."

"Well, I know one thing. He's ready to move on."

"Good. Now it's your job…"

"I know. To bridge the death of Vera and find Jason a wife and Angel a new mother."

"Exactly. How are those cooking lessons going?"

"I'm learning."

"Basketball?"

"Not yet. I think I'd be safer playing my harp."

Glory chuckled. Eliza noted that she'd never heard her mentor laugh.

"Go easy on yourself, Eliza. Pray to you know who and ask for strength."

"I will. I've got to get back to work. I'm cleaning the second floor today."

"How do you like cleaning?" Glory asked really curious to know.

"Well, it keeps your mind off some things."

"Good-bye, Eliza."

Eliza shut her cell phone and put it on her dresser. *Okay, Big Guy, this is the big conversation. I'm sorry I went against your wishes. It will not happen again. I pray you'll still let me see my parents. Amen.*

That night after dinner, Jason asked if everybody wanted a movie night. He'd picked out *Shrek*. Angel hopped around the kitchen. "Popcorn. We need popcorn, Daddy."

"Everyone go into the living room and get comfortable. I'll make the popcorn if Eliza will pour the soda."

Vera pulled herself up out of her chair. She grabbed her grandbaby's hand. "Let's get the best seats first."

Eliza knew her being alone with Jason, even for a few moments, was trouble. With Vera and Angel out of the way, he could ask her—whatever! She went to the fridge and grabbed a bottle of diet Coke. As she poured, Jason popped the popcorn in the air popper. Finally, Jason broke the silence. "I hope I didn't ruin our friendship last night, Eliza."

She sensed his sincerity immediately.

"But, you're a beautiful woman inside and out. You're the kind of woman I need in my life and Angel's life."

"I am in your life, Jason. Every day. You'll have me here to take care of all of you every day until you no longer need my services."

"But, I don't want you to look at it as services. I want more than that. I'm sorry. It's just that I have to be honest with myself and with you. I've wrestled with my conscious long enough. I now believe God has sent me someone special to be in my life and Angels'. I believe in God again, Eliza," he turned to look at her hoping to see her wanting him as much as he wanted her. Instead, she looked down and nervously continued pouring the soda.

"Let me pass out the sodas," Eliza grabbed three glasses.

"Subject dodged quite well."

Eliza made the mistake of looking back at him. She saw how sad he looked. She felt his hurt – real and genuine and stronger than she ever thought possible. Why her? Why did he want her out of all the women in the universe he could have?

"I'll meet you in the living room," when she got there, she saw exactly how Vera had arranged things. Eliza would have no choice but to sit next to Jason on the couch. The same couch where only last night they shared a passionate embrace, a heart stopping kiss. Jason entered the room with a big bowl of popcorn.

"We'll have to pass it around," he announced as he took his place next to Eliza.

Their arms brushed up against one another's, and Eliza thought she was going to die from want. She wanted his arm around her badly. She wanted to lay her head on his chest and curl up with him and watch the movie. Instead, she focused on what the donkey in the movie did.

Angel laughed throughout the entire movie. Vera did, too. Eliza admitted she had to laugh. Vera nodded at Eliza when Jason wasn't looking. Oooh, Eliza knew what that look meant. *His stinking mother still wanted to make them a couple.*

Jason picked up the bowl and two glasses and headed for the

kitchen. Eliza knew her job—clean up the rest, so she picked up the other glasses and went into the kitchen.

"Great movie, wasn't it?" Jason kept the conversation light. Eliza could handle that.

"I loved the donkey."

"Yeah. I always liked Eddie Murphy. It's a little bit later than I thought. Angel doesn't have to take a bath tonight. There's no school tomorrow."

"Do you need me to do anything else?"

"No, you've done enough for me already, Eliza. You'll never know just how much you've changed my life. Our lives."

"I'll go see to your mother."

"We're still on for tomorrow night? Skating, remember?"

Eliza didn't want to disappoint Angel, so she said the only thing she could. "Of course."

"Sleep well," to himself he added, "my other angel," Jason slowly made his way to his room. Once there, he picked up a picture of his deceased wife. "I'll always love you, Kathleen, but you knew. I need a wife, and Angel desperately needs a mother. I think God sent her to me. I hope you'll understand. I'll always make sure Angel knows how much her Mommy loved her, and when she's old enough, I'll tell her how she became our baby," Jason changed into a pair of boxers and collapsed onto the bed. He no longer felt like crying. He no longer felt alone, and that felt good. It felt right. He promised himself he'd take it slowly with Eliza since she acted so skittish, but he would be persistent and would never give up. One thing about him. When he knew something to be right for him or his family he pursued it relentlessly.

The next morning, Eliza did something she never did: she slept in late. She vaguely remembered hitting the alarm button off and rolling over to go back to sleep. At ten o'clock a knock on her door woke her.

"It's me, Eliza," Vera said loud enough for her to hear. Eliza jumped out of bed when she realized the time. She slipped into her robe and opened the door.

"I'm so sorry, Vera. I didn't mean to oversleep," Eliza genuinely apologized. Now she remembered the reason why she fell back into a deep slumber. The dream she had, had her feeling all sorts of new things. A dream filled with brown eyes and broad shoulders and gentle yet passionate kisses.

"No need to apologize, Child. We all sleep in every now and then. I think it's your body trying to tell you something. You needed your rest."

Eliza remembered how she thought that very thought about Vera. If the old woman only knew the dreams she'd had about her son, she'd be elated. Drat. Why couldn't she have what she wished for? Why couldn't she have Jason and Angel and Vera *and* her mother and father? Why was God putting her in a situation he had to know would be difficult for her? After all, He did know everything. He had to know Eliza would be attracted to Jason. Could it be the reason why Glory made it clear from the start that Jason was off limits? Why did she have to be an angel anyway? Why hadn't God sent her to the other side of heaven with her parents? Why? She had a million questions and no answers, just instructions to find Jason a wife and Angel a mother and make sure Vera crossed over all right. Heavenly life didn't make things fair. Just like earth life.

"Let me take a quick shower, and I'll be down to make breakfast," Eliza said as she picked out a pair of jeans and a blouse.

Vera laughed. "Breakfast has come and gone. But when you come downstairs they'll be some waffles with strawberries and whipped cream waiting for you."

"Well, at least let me walk you downstairs."

"No need to. I can see to that," Jason appeared in the doorway. He immediately sensed Eliza's discomfort.

"I'm sorry," she said running a hand through her tousled blond hair.

"No need for apologies. Mother's right, everyone needs to sleep in every now and then."

Double drat. He'd heard the whole conversation. She tried hard to concentrate but found it difficult with six foot something standing in her doorway in a pair of Levis and a white button down shirt with its sleeves rolled up exposing very masculine forearms. Since when had she taken to looking at forearms? Oh God, what a dither he had her in. She *had* to meet with Glory face-to-face—and soon!

Jason smiled at Eliza. She looked beautiful in the morning. As a matter-of-fact, she looked a whole lot like Angel. She could easily pass for her mother. "I'll take mother downstairs. You take your time showering."

"Thank you for being so understanding. It won't happen again," she said thinking to herself she couldn't guarantee Jason wouldn't slip into her dreams again.

A half hour later, Eliza stepped into the kitchen. Jason and Angel were playing tic tac toe while Vera watched. The minute she saw Eliza, she hopped up and grabbed the waffles. "I'll just heat these in the microwave. They'll be ready in a jiffy."

"Eliza, sit," the gentle command came from Jason. So Eliza did as told. She sat and waited while Vera, the woman she cared for, doted on her. She placed orange juice in front of her and a cup of freshly brewed coffee. Eliza sipped the coffee and let out a sigh. What good was it? Why fight her feelings? Maybe she should just tell Glory to pull her from this assignment. To get another angel who could resist a man like Jason Abbott.

"Now, you just let me know what you think of my homemade waffles," Vera said as she placed a heaping of waffles, strawberries and whipped cream in front of her. Against her will, Eliza's stomach growled.

"Hmmm. I think someone not only needs extra sleep, but needs some good food. Mom's waffles are the best," Jason drew a line through three x's much to Angel's dismay.

Vera winked at Eliza and sat down. "Eat, Girl, you've got some ice skating to do tonight. I have another special recipe for you to make for tonight, and when the three of you come home, I'll have hot chocolate and chocolate chip cookies ready for you."

"Another surprise dinner, Mom? Or can you clue us in so we can wait all day for dinnertime?"

"Meatloaf, mashed potatoes with garlic and green beans in gravy," Vera waited for a reaction and got the one she looked for.

"Yeah! I love your meatloaf grandma," Angel temporarily forgot that she'd just lost a game to her father.

"Yes, but Eliza's going to make it."

"Well, she's been duplicating your recipes perfectly so far, but meatloaf?" Jason rubbed his chin pretending to think about it, "Don't know if she can come close to yours, Mom."

Eliza took the bait. "Betcha I can," she crossed her arms over her chest. She didn't need his flirting, and she certainly didn't need to look across the table at Vera's smug expression. Only Angel seemed to be unaware of the tension in the room.

"Well dig in, Child. They're getting cold."

Eliza obeyed, and rewarded Vera with a groan from a pair of attractive lips. "These are heavenly."

"You'll learn to make those, too." Vera said. She certainly had more spunk the last few days. "I'll teach you next week because I plan on being around awhile. I'm feeling mighty good these past few days."

"Oh Grandma, I love you." Angel scrambled out of her chair and into her grandmother's arms.

"It's good to have you back, Mom," Jason said. Eliza sensed him getting all choked up. She also sensed his acute awareness of her. Somehow he knew how she felt about him and Angel and Vera. She knew because the *Big Guy* gave her extra in the sensory department, and for the four thousandth time she wondered if it wasn't a curse to know what people were feeling, but this, this thing with Jason, being able to read her, drove her nuts. *She* had the extra sensitive senses. Eliza reached across the table and took Vera's hand. "You look far different than the first time we met."

"Well, you were right. God is going to take me when he's ready not when the doctor's decide to stop chemotherapy. I'm glad I'm going to go in peace surrounded by those I love," Vera looked into Eliza's big blue eyes, "and that includes you."

Eliza felt touched by the admission. She had certainly worked in the right direction in bridging life to death, but that didn't mean

Angel and Jason would understand her death. She still had her work cut out for her. "I'll clean up, and if you don't mind," she turned to face Jason, "I have a friend from out of town that I have to meet with today. I won't be gone long—just a few hours."

"Eliza, your friends are welcome here."

"Well, we sort of already have plans to meet for lunch," Eliza hedged. Not exactly a total lie. She did intend to meet Glory at lunchtime in the park."

"Well, that's fine. As a matter of fact, you can take the entire day off. You've earned it."

His consideration touched Eliza and, yes, she felt that overwhelming feeling of attraction. Bill Wiggins had nothing on Jason. Bill Wiggins' feelings appeared to be child's play. Jason played in the all grown up field. "If you don't mind, I'll take you up on that, but I'll be back in time to make dinner," she addressed Vera.

"Be back by 3:30. That'll give us plenty of time to whip up my meatloaf."

Eliza excused herself and went back to her room. She needed some space, the only reason why she agreed to take time off. She needed to get her head *together...her feelings in check before tonight.* She also knew that although she'd enjoy skating with Jason and Angel, she'd be saddened by the fact that Robby no longer walked on this earth able to join her. Yes, she knew the little boy she'd cared for found happiness in heaven and no suffering, but she had strong feelings for those she cared for and missed them desperately. Not as desperately though as her parents. Just the thoughts of seeing them again made her reconsider her feelings for Jason. She quickly changed into a black sweater dress and black knee high boots. She opted for gold jewelry instead of pearls. She knew where to head: the mall. The one place where she could lose track of time. She loved shopping and browsing and people watching. Now, about her lunchtime meeting. Eliza plucked out her cell phone from her purse and rang Glory.

"I need to meet with you, Glory. There's so many things I'm feeling..."

"You can tell me over lunch."

"You don't want to meet in the park?"

"No, it's much too cold today. How about we meet at Riff's at noon?"

"I'll be there. Thank you, Glory."

"No need to thank me, that's why I'm here."

Well, now Eliza didn't tell a lie. She actually did have a luncheon date."

Eliza quietly slipped down the stairs. She didn't want to risk running into Jason. As she opened the closet door to retrieve her coat, Jason touched her on the shoulder. Eliza turned. She looked into those brown, brown eyes and felt herself being sucked into a place where only feelings mattered, not logic. She felt his eyes look her over and sensed his reaction to her outfit. He liked it – a lot! Before she had a chance to say anything, Jason spoke up.

"You look beautiful, Eliza. Are you meeting a boyfriend?"

Eliza wanted to lie and say yes, yes and stay away from me. Instead she said, "I told you, I don't have a boyfriend. I'm just meeting a girlfriend I've known for quite some time. She's only in for the day."

Jason frowned. "Then you don't have to go skating with us. Spend the time catching up with your friend."

For some reason, Eliza knew she should cheer and take him up on his offer, but felt let down instead. She didn't like the fact that he'd let her go so easily. "No, I'll be back at 3:30. I believe that's around the time Glory planned on heading back home."

Jason smiled. "Good. I would have hated not having you with us."

Eliza felt warm inside and felt a tingle up her arm when Jason lifted her hand and kissed the back of it.

"Have fun, and I'll see you at dinner."

Just as quietly as he had appeared, he disappeared down the long hall.

Eliza shrugged into her long black cashmere coat. She fixed her tam on her head and slipped on her warm fur-lined gloves. She didn't realize just how fashionable she looked, and she didn't realize that nobody would ever mistake her for an angel. Angels wore white and played the harp. They didn't walk through a crowded mall looking like something from *Glamour* magazine.

Eliza shivered as she warmed up her car. She had the heater on full blast. She could do without the cold weather. She'd have to mention that to Glory so her next assignment landed her in the tropics.

Eliza drove around the parking area and finally found a lone spot furthest from the elevator. "It'll have to do," she said to no one. She walked briskly toward the elevator. When she reached it, the doors opened. She hurried in along with six or seven other people. She found herself squished along the back wall. At least she didn't have to deal with the bitter cold of outside. When the elevator let out, Eliza immediately headed for Valley's department store. She wanted to look for a new sweater for the evening. As she cruised the aisles, she came upon the sweater section. Every kind of sweater imaginable beckoned to her. Then, she spotted it. High on the one wall hung a thick bright pink knitted sweater. It had buttons down the front. She immediately enlisted the help of a saleslady. Once she had the oversized sweater in her hand, she decided to buy a white turtleneck to go underneath as well as a pair of long johns. Pleased with her purchase, Eliza headed for the coffeehouse in the corner of the mall. She placed her purchases on the opposite chair and sat and read over the menu. When the waitress finally arrived, Eliza had decided on a chocolate expresso.

Deep in thought, the waitress interrupted her. "Would you care for a cinnamon bun? They're fresh from the oven."

"No thank you, I'll be meeting someone for lunch shortly."

The waitress walked away headed towards the kitchen. Eliza sighed as she sipped her hot drink. It felt good going down after having been out in the blustery cold. She soon found herself lost in thought. How to explain her feelings to Glory? She hadn't planned on being attracted to her new employer. In fact, as long as she'd been an angel, she'd never found herself attracted to any human or angelic male. She finished her drink and left her money on the table. Noon came quickly, and Riff's stood proudly across the street from the mall. It's rustic exterior looking like something out of a magazine. She bundled up dreading the blast of cold air that soon would follow.

Eliza opened the door to Riff's and felt the warm blast of air. She scanned the room looking for her mentor. Sure enough, Glory sat in a corner booth toward the back. Good. They would have privacy. She made her way over to the booth, unbuttoning her coat at the same time. When she reached Glory's table, she shrugged out of her coat but left on her tam.

"My, don't we look like the fashion plate," Glory said.

"Oh, thanks. It's an outfit I picked up over the years."

"Yes, and there have been many years to do so. Eliza, The Chief knows you've been serving him for a long time now. Please feel free to discuss anything you want."

"Fine. I think I'm falling in love with a man I'm not supposed to fall in love with," there. She'd put it right there on the table for Glory. No beating around the bush for her.

"I see. We thought that might be a problem."

"Well, if you thought that might be a problem why didn't you just put someone else on the case?"

"The Chief specifically requested you for this assignment. I don't know his reasons though, I admit, I questioned Him myself."

"And he said?"

Glory became quiet. "Well, no I didn't actually question Him directly. I just questioned Him in my heart. I thought it unfair to put you in such a difficult situation."

"Thank you. At least you understand. Glory, I love little Angel with my whole heart. And Vera – well, she's the closest thing I've had to a mother in a long time."

"And Jason?" just as Glory asked the question a waiter appeared with two menus.

"Ladies, the special of the day is a lobster bisque soup and mushrooms stuffed with crabmeat. Our entrees are broiled haddock done in a light butter and garlic sauce and lobster primavera. Both are $14.99, and I might add both are delicious. I've sampled them myself."

"Could we have a few minutes?" Eliza asked. She wanted to continue her conversation with Glory. She wanted to get to the heart of things.

"Certainly. Take your time," the waiter walked away leaving a dead silence between the two women.

Finally, it was Glory who spoke. "You can be honest with me. Maybe that will help."

"Jason has strong, overwhelming feelings for me. I *feel* it – powerfully. When I'm in the room with him, I sometimes forget to breathe. I've never met anyone like him. He's so strong and caring and good. If I hadn't died in that car crash and lived to meet Jason, I would have wanted him for a husband and father of my children."

There. She laid out all her cards.

"I'm sorry, Eliza. The only guidance I've been told to give you is to tell you to keep your relationship with Jason platonic. I don't know the reason. I only know that if you choose not to, you won't see your parents. I know it sounds cruel. I wonder myself…"

"It is cruel," Eliza said angrily, "and totally unfair. I've done everything I've ever been told to do, and I've always put my whole heart and soul into whatever assignment given. Why? Why would He deny me seeing my parents? I've done everything… everything He's asked of me." Now Eliza sounded more sad than angry.

"Eliza," Glory put her hand over Eliza's hand. "He must have a reason – a very good reason for doing this. The Chief's not cruel. He's loving and caring and wants to see his children happy."

"Then he'd let me see my parents assignment or not," Eliza interrupted.

"Oh please, Eliza, don't tell me you're turning on God."

A tear managed to escape and make it's way down Eliza's delicately beautiful face. "No, no, I'm not turning on Him. I'm questioning Him. Isn't it all right to question what you don't understand? *I've* never met Him."

"I have, Eliza. Believe me, He's all about love and sharing and giving and kindness," the waiter returned.

"Ladies, have you decided?"

"Yes, I'll have the lobster bisque and lobster primavera," Eliza answered.

"I'll have the same," Glory added.

"Excellent choice, ladies. I'll have your soup in a few minutes."

"Eliza, can you just trust The Chief to know what's in your best interest? Love Jason and Angel and Vera, but don't get romantically attached to Jason."

"Fine," Eliza's shoulders drooped in defeat. Disappointed because her mentor didn't give her the green light with Jason, Eliza resigned herself to a life without romance. On the bright side, she'd get to visit with her parents. She just didn't understand why she couldn't have both. "I know my assignment and will carry it out. Vera's not a problem, and I believe I can help Jason and Angel cope with Vera's eventual passing. As for finding Jason a wife – I'll start looking tonight."

"Tonight?" Glory raised an eyebrow.

"Tonight when the three of us go ice skating. I'll be on the look out for women I feel are attracted to Jason and are worthy of his affections."

Glory lowered her eyes. She couldn't look Eliza straight in the eye as she said, "I think that's a good idea."

"Consider it done. But I want you to know, that if I had my Christmas wish, it would be to be with Jason and his family *and* see my parents."

At that moment the waiter appeared with their soup. After he left, Glory said, "Let's enjoy lunch, Eliza. I don't see much of you anymore."

This time, Eliza reached out for Glory's hand. "I know it's not your doing. You're only following instructions given you. Let's lighten the conversation a bit, eh? Like how are some of my favorite people doing in heaven?"

Relieved, Glory went on to tell Eliza all about Robby and the other children and families she had worked with over the years.

"My, this dish is quite tasty. I haven't had good food in a long time. It's nice to sometimes eat human food."

Eliza laughed. "This restaurant has nothing on Vera. Why, she could open her own restaurant," after she said the words a *ding* sounded in her brain. Maybe Vera could give her recipes to a talented chef and Jason could fund the costs of a start up venture. She'd have to think some more on that idea.

"Eliza, I've had a wonderful time. I love you and care about you and love working with you. I'll pray you have the strength to do the right thing."

"Thank you," Eliza said as she put on her coat, "I dread going back out in this blasted weather. Which reminds me, could you see to it that my next assignment is in the Bahamas?"

Glory laughed, "I'll do my best."

The two women parted at the front door. Eliza put up her collar and rushed across the street. It just started to snow. Once inside the mall, she breathed a sigh of relief. She knew the score. Glory knew how she felt. If nothing else she could be honest with her feelings though not act on them. As she walked through the mall she smiled. The beautiful domed building showcased gaily-decorated Christmas wreaths and candy canes and dozens of miniature white lights. Santa sat in the center of it all hoisting one child after another onto his lap for a picture. It made her wonder if Jason planned on taking Angel for her picture with Santa Claus. She'd have to remind him.

Eliza looked at her watch. It read 2:05. Well, she had an hour and a half to kill. She started by going to the all men's store. She wandered around the store until she came to the aftershave section. She couldn't help herself. She sniffed a half dozen bottles and found one she couldn't resist buying for Jason. She'd just have to add it to his Christmas present. No rule against that. At least she could indulge herself in that way.

After wandering around the mall and browsing in all the boutiques and department stores for more than an hour, she decided to go home.

Home. Why did the Abbott's house start to feel like home? She'd never felt that with any other family she'd been involved with. She made a mad dash to her car and started it up. Unfortunately, it took a good ten minutes before the heater kicked in. As she drove back to Cherry Street, she wondered how to control her feelings and, more importantly, put a damper on Jason's.

Eliza entered the house with the key Jason had given her. The quiet unnerved her. She peeked in the kitchen to no avail. No Vera. No Angel. No Jason. She hung up her coat and hat, stuffed her gloves in her coat pocket and carried her purchase back to her room. Once inside she took out the pink sweater and snuggled into it. Warm and soft and oh so feminine best described it. She placed it on the bed with the white turtle neck and long underwear and pulled out a pair of worn jeans. She also managed to find her white gloves. Whala! The perfect outfit for a night of indoor ice skating. Then, she proceeded to Vera's room. She had only to knock on the door once for an answer.

"Come in," a strong voice answered. A man's voice not an elderly woman's. She opened the door and came face to face with Jason.

"How did your day go?" he asked smiling at her.

"Perfect. I needed to talk to an old friend."

"Well, Mom had her nap and is dying to show you how to make her meatloaf even though I have my doubts about your duplicating this particular dish. Dad's favorite, by the way."

"Yes, well I have a good student in Eliza. I think you'll all be shocked by how good it turns out."

Eliza looked at Jason. "Exactly. Let's get started, shall we, Vera?"

"I'll leave you women to your cooking while I check in on Angel."

"Where is Angel?" Eliza asked.

"She's in her room playing with her dolls."

"I thought she kept all her dolls downstairs in the room with the tree?" a puzzled Eliza questioned.

"Yes, well now that she likes her room, she's been moving some of her toys up here."

Eliza smiled, and so did Jason. The smile stopped her heart briefly. "I guess our little munchkin is getting used to her bedroom."

"Thanks to you," Jason said. He walked out the door and down the hall to his daughter's bedroom.

"Well now, tell me all about your day. Who is this friend from out of town?" a definitely nosy Vera asked.

"Glory. She's been a friend of mine for a long, long time–since my parents died."

"Well I'm glad to see you have someone in this world to help you out. You know we would do anything for you after all you've done for us," Vera slowly rose from the bed.

"But I haven't done anything except my job, Vera," a humble Eliza responded.

"Pooh! You've made my life brighter and my belief in God stronger, and you've helped Angel sleep through the nights by herself like any six-year-old should be doing. As for Jason…"

Eliza didn't want to hear it, so she cut Vera off. "Let's go make that meatloaf."

Vera understood Eliza's mixed feelings about her son. After all, she knew he loved his beloved Kathleen very much. Vera also knew that she tried to make Eliza understand that she knew her baby boy had feelings for Eliza much more powerful than he'd ever had for Kathleen. The question remained on how to get them together. Tonight would be a start. She wouldn't be in the way of the trio of skaters.

"Yes, let's show Jason you can make a meatloaf that tastes like mine," Vera winked, and Eliza rolled her eyes.

"Isn't it funny how we know it's going to taste *exactly* like yours?"

"Hmmm. What he doesn't know won't hurt him. Besides, I'm going to be teaching you how."

That's when Eliza remembered her idea. "Vera," she said excitedly, "what would you think about opening a restaurant?"

Vera just looked at Eliza for a few minutes. "You do know I'm dying. I might be in remission, but Eliza, I have cancer."

"Well maybe you could hire someone who could really duplicate your recipes. It could be a down home cooking themed restaurant."

"Maybe you could learn the recipes and Jason could back it," Vera said slyly.

"No, I can't cook. You above all people know that. I mean, wouldn't it be great to have a local restaurant named after you–Vera's Place."

"Eliza, if I knew my days weren't numbered, I'd jump on the idea. I do love so to cook and welcome and greet people, but Child, you have to remember, just like Jason does, that I'm not for this earth for that much longer. I've been given a reprieve, and I believe it's so I see my son happily married again."

"Well I'll be working on that tonight."

"What's that supposed to mean?" Vera cautiously inquired. She didn't want to get her hopes up.

Not to worry, Eliza doused the fire.

"I'm going to start looking for a wife for him and good mother for Angel. I'll help him find someone who can take care of them."

"I think *I've* already found the wife and mother, but she's a stubborn fool," Vera hmphed.

Eliza put her arm around the older woman. "No, Vera. I'm not the woman he needs, but I'll promise you I'll see to it that he gets the best wife and mother on the face of this earth."

"Let's go make that meatloaf," Vera walked off toward the stairs.

"Here, let me help you," Eliza said offering Vera her arm.

"No," Vera turned on her, "Let me help you. My son and grandbaby are exactly what you need in your life, and it just so happens you're exactly what they need. Why you don't see it, I don't know, but I do know this. My son hasn't looked at another woman the way he does you. Not even his Kathleen. You're his soul mate. I know it. Here," Vera said as she thumped her heart.

Two hours later a surprised Jason gobbled up two plates of meatloaf. "I guess you really are my mother's match."

"Hmmm. And you didn't think I could do it. That ought to teach you. Now, you and Angel go get ready for skating while I clean up. Then I'll slip into my skating attire."

Eliza felt Vera's hand on her arm. "Let me clean up so you can get ready. I'm really feeling quite well."

"Are you sure…" Eliza started to ask.

"Absolutely. I'd tell you if I couldn't handle it."

"Okay. Thanks," she bent down and kissed Vera on the cheek. Jason didn't miss the action. Eliza again started getting overwhelming feelings of longing. "I'll be down in a few minutes, Jason," she took off for the steps before he could reply.

Once in her room, Eliza slipped into her old jeans and new attire. She looked in the mirror. For the first time, she realized she could pass for Angel's mother. She went downstairs and waited in a now spic-and-span clean kitchen–Vera no where in sight.

"Eliza, Eliza, we match!" Angel came bounding into the room. "I've got on my pink sweater, too!"

"And don't you look beautiful in it."

"I hope as beautiful as you," Angel answered honestly.

"Absolutely," Jason entered the room, "I'll have the two most beautiful women on my arm tonight," he looked at Eliza, "Mom's in her room watching a movie. Ever see *The Bishop's Wife?*"

Eliza knew the movie by heart. She knew every angel movie out there, but that particular one made a point that she herself now needed to remember: When an angel starts to have romantic feelings toward a human it is a danger sign. A sign to move on never to return. The thought of never seeing Jason and Angel again made her sad. She'd just have to enjoy what time was given. "I know the movie. It's one of my Christmas favorites. Now, what do you say we go skating?"

CHAPTER TWELVE

Jason held Angel's mittened hand as the three of them walked from the parking lot to the skating arena. Still snowing lightly, it made everything seem like it was coated in powdered sugar–a real life winter wonderland just like inside the Christmas shakers. Even though Eliza hated the cold weather, something about snow made Christmas even more special. She'd cross her fingers that it would snow Christmas Eve.

Jason insisted on paying for the skating tickets and rental skates. Eliza just looked at it as her boss paying her for her time. She couldn't allow herself to think of it as a *date*.

"Here, let me lace these up for you," Eliza said as she tied Angel's skates. She then did her own and waited patiently for Jason to finish.

"When's the last time you were on ice?" Jason asked Eliza.

"About a year ago. I used to skate with Robby every weekend. He had a Wilms Tumor. He died a few weeks before you and I met."

"I'm sorry," Jason said. The sincerity oozing from him made Eliza long for things she couldn't have, "It can't be easy taking care of terminal patients."

"Actually, it's not so bad when you know you're helping make their life better until they cross over to the other side."

"Is that how you see it? As another side? No heaven in the sky?" Jason questioned Eliza.

"Yes. I think we're all souls who return home one day. On the other side there's no pain, only unconditional love. I also believe some souls come back to earth to learn lessons they didn't learn in their previous life. And some may even go on to become angels guiding humans in need of help."

"That's pretty specific beliefs."

"I'm a pretty specific person."

Angel, who had been listening to the entire conversation added her opinion. "I think God takes us all to heaven to be with him and it's like a big party because you get to be with all of your family and friends again."

Eliza knelt beside Angel. "I'm sure you're right. Take my hand, and we'll show your Dad just how well we skate."

Angel latched onto Eliza. Jason kept two paces behind the two blondes that meant the world to him. Soon, Eliza guided Angel on the ice.

"Hey, I'm beginning to feel left out," Jason skated up behind Eliza.

"Then grab onto Angel's other hand. We'll see how well you can keep up," Eliza laughed, and Jason felt like he'd been hit in the gut. This woman, who'd only recently come into their lives, had the power to make him feel things he'd never felt before. Not even with Kathleen.

So the three of them skated around the arena time after time laughing and singing Christmas carols at the tops of their lungs. Other skaters merely smiled at the happy threesome who looked like a family. After an hour of making many laps around the arena, Eliza broke free. She needed to feel free so she skated with all her heart. Jason and Angel watched in awe as Eliza did triple axles and jumps and turns. Ever since Robby, she'd felt skating made her lose all self-consciousness. She could just glide gracefully on the ice until she could forget why she had to spend time there–to make a dying boy happy.

When Eliza skated back to Jason and Angel, a round of applause sounded. A group of people had stopped skating to watch Eliza. Eliza blushed and did a little curtsy. Once the crowd broke up, Jason put his arm beneath hers. "Another talent I see, and we thought you could only cook and play harp."

"Never underestimate a woman, Jason."

"I'm beginning to see," he slid her gloved fingers between his as Angel skated on his other side, "What do you say we call it a night and go back home for chocolate chip cookies and hot chocolate?"

"Yeah, Daddy! I had fun!"

"We'll come back again, Pumpkin," Jason tweaked Angel on the nose.

Soon the threesome got back in Jason's car and headed for the large Victorian that Eliza now thought of as home. By now, the snow had stopped and the temperatures were up a few degrees. They piled out of the car laughing at one of Angel's jokes. Vera stood in the doorway just nodding. They needed more time alone as a family she realized, and she felt determined not to get in the way.

"Come on now, let's hang up your coats while I put on the hot chocolate," to Eliza she added, "I don't use the packets from the grocery store. I make mine from scratch.

Eliza smiled. "Somehow it wouldn't seem right if you didn't, but I hope you have some whipped cream in the fridge."

"I do. I do," Vera hustled down the hallway and into the oversized kitchen. Three hungry people followed, "Sit. Sit," Vera ordered, and all three listened dutifully.

"Mmmm. Something smells good, Grandma," Angel fidgeted in her seat.

Vera opened the oven and took out a tray of freshly baked oversized chocolate chip cookies. "I put beer in the batter to make them a bit more fluffy," she said aside to Eliza. Eliza wondered if she'd ever remember all these recipes. "Now let them cool a bit before you dive right into them," Vera ordered.

A few minutes later all three were ooohing and ahhhing over the cookies and cocoa.

"I guess I'll be getting a lesson on these," Eliza smiled at Vera. Vera now had color in her cheeks–a far cry from when they met.

"Now, I'm going to bed, but you three stay up and watch a movie or play a game. I'm tuckered out from baking."

"I'll help you up the stairs, Mom," Jason stood right by Vera's side.

"I'd like that, Son. Goodnight to all," she bent over and kissed the top of Angel's head, "and you, young lady, sleep well like you have been."

"Oh Grandma, I'm not afraid anymore. I say the angel prayer Eliza taught me."

Vera looked back at Eliza and thought for the hundredth time how right Eliza could be for her family, "Goodnight, Eliza."

"Goodnight, Vera. I'll see you bright and early in the morning. No sleeping in tomorrow."

Once back in the sanctuary of her room, Eliza slipped into her softest pajamas. It felt good to be back on the ice. It also made her wonder about Robby. Did he finally get to be with his grandparents? Or, did The Big Guy Upstairs decide to send him to angel school, too? She made a mental note to ask Glory next time they spoke. Eliza set her alarm for 6 a.m. and she covered herself with the down comforter and velour blankets. She snuggled against her pillows and fell into a deep sleep. At 2 o'clock she awoke frantic. She had dreamed Jason's death. An intruder in his house shot him. Eliza, now fully awake, realized it had been just a dream and her imagination working overtime, but it left her with an odd feeling. For someone who understood death meant not an ending but a beginning free from pain and restraints of earth life, she didn't accept death all that well. Again, she wondered why she couldn't be reunited with her parents now. Maybe that had something to do with her feelings toward death. She looked at it from the viewpoint of missing people you love. She could just hear Glory saying that's why she got this assignment–because she could relate to what Jason and Angel would feel when Vera passed over. She also wondered if she'd get a chance to see Vera once back in heaven. For an angel, she sure didn't know much, and it seemed Glory wasn't completely sure of everything either. Maybe God's plan to reunite her with her parents would only be for a brief time and then He'd send her back down to earth as an angel. Or, maybe, she'd be a mentor, like Glory, to a younger angel. She could understand that because at least she'd see her parents one more time and would be able to tell them how much she loved and missed them. She'd get to see how happy they could be together in heaven instead of on an earth that didn't always make life easy. Eliza thought about skating with Angel and Jason. That thought left her feeling warm and happy inside, and soon she drifted back to sleep.

Come six a.m., she went to get Vera but noticed the door was wide open with no sign of the older woman. She decided to go downstairs in her pajamas to see if she should dress for church. She didn't know the family's routine with that. As she approached the kitchen delightful smells of cinnamon and fresh baking dough filled the air. She inhaled and released a contented sigh.

"And I thought it was you creating all those good smells," Jason came up from behind Eliza. She felt a bit self-conscious without her robe, then decided that was silly. After all, she wore less on the beach. Not even a thought or two later, she decided herself wrong with that assessment. She could *feel* how Jason found her beautiful. She could *feel* how he wanted to hold her, and she could *feel* his feelings had nothing to do with being platonic.

"I just wanted to ask Vera if she'd like to go to church with me. I'm not quite sure how to dress," Eliza said as she pulled on the bottom of her pajama top.

"Actually, I planned on asking you to join us this morning. Mass at St. Peter's is at nine. The ladies tend to get pretty dressed up–dresses and skirts."

"Will Vera be going?"

"That I don't know because I haven't talked to her, yet. I'm sure I'll take her by surprise considering I haven't stepped foot in a church since Kathleen died."

"Oh," Eliza didn't know what to say, but she could *feel* how at ease he was mentioning Kathleen's name.

Together they entered the kitchen. When Vera saw them side-by-side, she gave them a big smile. "Sit, the cinnamon coffee cake is almost done. Eliza, if you wouldn't mind putting the coffee on, I'd sure appreciate it."

"No problem, Vera. Then, I think I'll go change into something suitable for church."

"Pish. You stay just like you are. You can go upstairs and change when you've finished my breakfast."

"Mom, I'm taking Angel and Eliza to nine o'clock mass at St. Peter's. Would you like to join us?"

Now Vera practically beamed, her smile so bright. "What's made you change your mind about returning to the church?" she asked though she knew the answer.

"I've finally come to terms with things that have happened, are happening, in my life. I also happen to think Angel should grow up with a religious background of some sort."

"Son, if you give me time to put on my Sunday best, I'll be pleased to join the three of you."

"Well, let me escort you upstairs," Eliza said pouring coffee in hers and Jason's mugs, "I'll help you dress, too."

"Only if you promise to come back down and eat breakfast with my son."

Eliza knew she'd never win these matchmaking spells, so she went along with it. "Absolutely, I can't wait to dig into your coffee cake. I'll wake Angel on my way back down."

Sure enough, a few minutes later, Eliza returned hand-in-hand with Angel. Angel immediately plopped into her seat and asked for some of the coffee cake that Jason had put in the center of the table. "I'll get you some juice unless you'd like chocolate milk?"

"Chocolate milk, please, Eliza," Jason cut a slice of cake and place it on his baby girl's plate, and Eliza put a glass of chocolate milk in front of her."

"Angel, we're all going to church this morning," Jason knew his daughter didn't remember anything about church, and he certainly hadn't told her. Besides those few prayers, Angel drew a blank when it came to going to church.

"Yes, so you can thank God for sending his angels to protect you,"

Eliza said as she sat across from Jason.

"Okay. Do I have to wear my school uniform?"

"No, Sweetheart, but you do have to get dressed up real pretty. Eliza can even put a matching bow in your hair."

Angel's eyes lit up. "Can I wear my pink and white dress that floats on the air when I twirl around?"

"Sure, Pumpkin."

Now Angel beamed all ears and eyes. "I have a pretty bow and shoes that go with that dress, Eliza."

"Well, after breakfast we'll get you all gussied up."

Angel quickly wolfed down her breakfast. She held out her hand to Eliza. "Let's go," the enthusiastic little girl said.

Eliza looked at Jason. "Don't worry, I'll clean up, but you'll owe me a super fantastic dinner."

"I'll think on that. Maybe your mother can come up with something unusual."

Eliza and Angel made their way upstairs to Angel's room. Eliza picked up the picture of Kathleen. "You miss her, huh?"

Angel shook her head. "Yes, but I was too little to really remember anything about her–only what Daddy tells me."

"You can say a special prayer for her when you're in church. In fact, you can light a candle for her. That's a way of saying you love someone who has passed away and hoping they're happy in heaven."

Angel nodded. "Good. Then, I'll light two candles, one for my grandpa so that he lives in heaven with my grandma, and one for my Mommy."

The rest of the time, Angel remained quite. She seemed deep in thought. Once Eliza had her dress on and bow in her hair, Angel twirled around and around, giggling as she did. Eliza smiled. This child had wormed her way into her heart more so than Robby or any of the others. "Come on, let's find me a suitable dress," Angel latched on to Eliza's hand. Jason bumped into them at the stairs to check on his mother.

"My, aren't we all grown-up, and beautiful, too!"

"See, Daddy," Angel said as she twirled around.

"I think you're going to get dizzy if you keep doing that," Jason said with a laugh. He looked at Eliza, "I'm just checking on Mom, then I'll get dressed in my Sunday finery. Though God knows what it might look like."

"Jason?" Eliza ventured, "I think this is a good thing for Angel and your Mom."

"I'm sure you're right. For the first time in a long time, I feel I have many blessings to be grateful for. I just hadn't been paying attention to them—until you."

Eliza decided to ignore his last remark, but she *felt* it–that overwhelming sense of love and contentment and now a sense of peace. "Angel, let's find me a dress."

Angel wasted no time in throwing open Eliza's closet doors.

"Oh, Eliza, this pink and white one is so pretty, and it'll match mine. Please wear it, please?"

"Oh, all right," she said. She'd do anything for Angel. Besides, the pink dress looked nice on her accentuating her small waist and blonde hair. She changed while Angel looked on.

"Don't those stockings feel funny?"

"No, and I'm sure you'll be wearing tights and stockings soon enough."

"I like my lacy socks."

"Yes, but in the winter your little legs will get cold."

"Then, we'll have to buy a pair for me tomorrow when we go Christmas shopping. You haven't forgotten?"

"No," Eliza squeezed her cheeks, "I never forget important things like that. I also happen to think a few pair of tights are a good idea. We'll talk to your father about it."

Eliza and Angel met Jason and Vera in the tree room. They had an hour to kill so Jason suggested playing Candyland. Finally, the clock read twenty to nine.

"We best be going if we're not to stand in the back," Vera said.

The four of them snuggled into their warmest coats and headed off for Sunday mass.

Eliza made sure she sat on the end with Angel by her side. Jason followed then Vera. She said a few prayers and decided now was a good time to ask God for a favor. "Dear God, let me have Jason and his family along with my family. It's my Christmas wish. Amen," she glanced sideways at Jason and saw him deep in thought as he read from the misselette at times, by heart at other times. He hadn't been that far gone from God, after all.

During the homily, Eliza couldn't help thinking God tried sending her an answer to her prayers. The priest expounded on how God always answered prayers, but not always in the way asked. He cited an example of a man who prayed he win a trip. When he lost he thought God didn't answer his prayers. However, the man later learned the plane he would have been on crashed and all of the passengers died. The priest's point stated that God did indeed answer prayers in his own way and for reasons we can't always understand. Though sometimes we can look back at unanswered prayers and see how, in fact, they might have been much like the man praying for a trip.

After church, a few of Vera's friends complimented her on how nice she looked and made small talk. When they left, Vera said in an aside to Eliza, "When they found out I was dying from cancer they wanted no part of me. Too afraid of facing death. Oh, I don't hold it against them, but it sure would be nice to have company every now and then."

Eliza's bells went off. "Who are they Vera?"

"Emily Robertson, Mary Hart and Doris Weathers. I used to play cards with them every Tuesday night."

Eliza already had a plan formulating in her mind about the coming Tuesday. She'd just need a little help from Jason to make it happen.

Once back in the spotless Victorian, Vera reminded Eliza they'd have early afternoon dinner. Jason begged off saying he had some work to catch up with, and Angel told them she planned on going to her room to play with her dolls. When Jason and Angel were out of site, Eliza asked, "What are we making for dinner?"

"Why roast beef with mashed potatoes and creamed corn."

"Will I be able to help?"

"Eliza, this recipe is so easy even Angel could do it."

"Then, get me an apron. I don't want to ruin my Sunday best, but I also feel like staying dressed up… something about Sundays."

"I know exactly what you mean. When Kathleen was alive we all stayed in our finery and would go for a long ride after dinner."

"You miss her a lot, too," a simple statement. Sometimes when talking to Vera about Kathleen, she got a deep sense of caring.

"You know I do. She made a wonderful daughter-in-law and mother to that child."

"Not to change the subject, but shouldn't we get started on that roast beef?"

Vera proceeded to the refrigerator. She had let the meat thaw overnight. "First we brown it in olive oil, then we add this box of onion soup and water and let it cook a few hours. The longer you do, the more tender the meat. You can peel and cut potatoes."

The two women worked together talking about everything and nothing.

Later, Vera called to Jason and Angel.

"I'll go get Daddy," Angel yelled down the stairs.

During dinner Jason dropped the bomb. "I think it's time we go to the pound and find you a dog."

Angel almost jumped out of her seat. "Daddy, Daddy! Can we really?"

"Really. I think today's as good a day as any. Eliza?"

"Don't look at me. I told Angel I had no problem caring for a dog when you hired me."

"Then it's settled."

Vera decided she'd sit this one out. She wanted to see the three of them alone and making such a big decision. "I think I'll stay home and be surprised."

Jason immediately appeared concerned. He had no idea his mother played matchmaker. "Do you not feel well?"

"No. I just need a little rest."

Eliza instantly sensed Vera's motivation. She figured she couldn't do anything about it, and she couldn't be mad at her either.

126

The three of them entered the local dog pound. A young girl immediately approached them. "Can I help you?"

"We're in the market for a puppy," Jason said.

Angel nodded her head vehemently. Eliza just stood in the background taking it all in.

"Well, to tell you the truth, we don't have any puppies. They're always the first to go. It's the older dogs we have trouble placing, and if we can't…" the girl left the rest unspoken aware of Angel's listening to the conversation.

"You could go in the pound and look around. You just might see a dog you like," she addressed Angel.

"Pumpkin?"

"Okay, Daddy. I want to see the dogs."

They walked around the cages. A couple dogs took to Angel, but it wasn't until she found the golden retriever that she got excited. She put her hand in the cage, and the dog licked her fingers.

"Him, Daddy. I want him."

The dog barked as almost to say, "Take me home with you."

"Well, let's check with the girl."

"Oh, sir, we just got him in yesterday. The owner couldn't keep him because her little girl had an allergic reaction to the dog. He's only nine months old so he's still a puppy," she looked at Angel on that last line.

"What do we have to do?"

"Just fill out these papers. We'll do a background check. We also take care of the shots and neutering. We just asked for a sixty dollar donation to keep the pound going."

"Fine, let's get started."

On the way home in the car, Angel acted like seventh heaven had arrived. "I think I'm going to name him Sunshine."

"Why Sunshine, Angel?" Eliza queried.

"Because we got him on a sunny day!"

Jason looked at Eliza in the rearview mirror and winked. Eliza smiled. Both father and daughter felt pleased with themselves. Soon Eliza would be paper training a dog. She couldn't wait to tell Glory this one.

"Will we have him in time for Christmas, Daddy?"

"I'm sure we'll have him in a few days."

"Goody-goody gumdrops. Wait till grandma sees him."

Jason pulled up in front of his home. Angel hopped right out and raced to the door. Once inside she yelled, "Grandma, grandma, where are you?"

No answer. "She's probably in her room," Jason said. "I'll go for her and meet you in the tree room."

When Eliza first entered the room, she didn't see Vera because of the darkness with only the tree lights flicking on and off. Then, she spotted her. Vera lie on the floor next to the couch.

"Oh, Vera. What happened?" Eliza knelt next to her.

Vera sounded weak with her reply. "I just missed the couch is all. A weak spell. I guess I've been overdoing it. Help me up, Dear, and please don't tell Jason."

"No," Eliza's said in a firm voice, "Jason has to know how you're doing. Vera, it won't do Jason and Angel any good to live in a fantasy world. They have to learn to accept you may not be long for this earth even though you've been feeling better."

"You're right," a sheepish Vera answered, "I guess I should be preparing them for my death."

"Vera, we've all been walking around here the past few days like everything is normal. It's not. You're in remission. That doesn't mean you're cured."

I know. I know," Vera said as Eliza helped her to the couch.

"Did you hurt anything?"

"Only my hand. I landed on it kind of funny."

"Let me see it," Eliza gently ordered.

Vera obeyed. She held out her injured hand.

"It just looks like it's bruised–nothing serious, but consider yourself lucky this time. You could have broken something."

"Who could have broken something?" Jason marched into the room followed by Angel. He had a big smile on his face.

"Your mother fell trying to sit on the couch."

Immediately, Jason's smile changed to a firm line. "Mom, what happened."

"I had a little weak spell."

"I knew you were overdoing it. From now on, Mom, you're going to take it easy and always have someone with you."

Vera tried to protest to no avail. Angel remained strangely quiet. Jason guided Eliza into the kitchen by the arm. "Do you think the cancer is back?"

"Jason, she fell. That doesn't mean anything other than she's weaker than we thought, but I'm not going to lie to you–it could be back and making her weak. You have to prepare yourself for her death. She is dying, Jason. It's a fact you have to accept. I love your mother, but I also am a realist. You've also got to prepare Angel for her grandmother's death."

"I'll take her to the doctor's tomorrow morning. Can you take Angel to school?"

"Certainly. I could meet you there after I drop her off."

"That's not necessary. It's something I have to do by myself."

Eliza knew why. She felt the tears that didn't fall. "Let's go back in there and watch a movie."

"No, I want mother to go to bed and rest."

"Whatever you say."

"You don't agree with me?" Jason looked at Eliza as though not really seeing her.

"I agree it would be the wiser choice."

"Could you talk to Angel for me... you know, kind of set the stage for what I have to tell her?"

Eliza put her hand on his forearm. The minute she touched him, she *felt* that warm, fuzzy feeling she always got, and she sensed Jason felt the same way. Even distracted by the feelings and by looking into his deep, brown, caring eyes, she replied, "I'll talk to her for you, Jason. I'll do what I can."

Jason impulsively leaned down and kissed Eliza's cheek, "thank you for being our angel." Then, he left the room.

Eliza just stood there thinking about his last words. If only he knew...

Angel tugged on Eliza's sleeve. "Is grandma going to be okay?"

Eliza pulled out a chair and motioned her to sit. "I'm not going to lie to you, Angel. You're a big girl, and you deserve the truth. Honey, your grandmother is a very sick person. She's better some days than others."

"I know, one day she'll be in heaven with the angels. Is it going to be soon, Eliza?"

Eliza reached down and hugged the little girl with the blonde curls so like her own. "Nobody knows the answer to that. Nobody that is but God. When God is ready to take her to his home, he will, and we'll all be very, very sad, but in heaven she won't be sick anymore, and she'll be with your Mom and Grandpa."

A tear trickled down Angel's cheek. The first time she'd seen Angel cry. The little girl had been such a trooper. "I'll miss Grandma. If something happens to my Daddy would you take care of me, Eliza?"

Eliza got mixed vibes from Angel. Some seemed like sadness another part fear. "Oh, Angel, yes I would take care of you, but your Daddy is going to live a real long time."

"But, you said only God knows when a person has to go to heaven."

Eliza bit her lip. True, but she didn't want to scare the child. "Well, usually when you're young, like your father, it takes a long time to die."

"But, my Mommy died young."

This stumped Eliza. Thankfully, Jason entered the room, her cue to leave. She kissed Angel goodnight and fled to the safety of her room. She took out her cell phone. She had a few questions for Glory.

CHAPTER THIRTEEN

"Glory, how do you deal with a frightened six-year-old who is wise for her years?"

"You mean, Angel?"

"Of course I mean Angel," she let out an exasperated sigh. "I don't mean to be short with you, but it just bugs me that I don't have all the answers. Here I am an angel who's been to heaven, but I can't tell a child that her father can't die at a moment's notice."

"She's afraid of her father dying?"

"Yes. Glory, all she's know from a young age is death. She's accepted it, but she's terrified that her father is going to be taken from her. I *feel* her fear something fierce."

"Well, what have you told her?"

"I told her that he would be around a long, long time and that usually people as young as her father don't die. Know what she said? My Mommy died young. I just don't know how to make her understand she can't live in fear of everyone dying. She even asked me if I would take care of her if her father did die."

"And you said?"

"Of course! I would never leave that precious little girl alone on this earth."

"Even if it meant never seeing your mother and father?"

Eliza sighed again. "Yes, even if it meant that. I love her to pieces and would want her safe and well cared for. I don't think I'd trust anyone other than myself to take care of her."

"So then your love for this little girl is more than your just having feelings for her father." The statement hung in the air. Glory to mean it to be a question.

"Again, yes. I feel like I'm her mother. I can't help it that I fell in love with Jason, Vera, too. Glory there has to be a reason why God put me here knowing I would be sorely tempted to not follow orders."

"The important thing is that you are, Eliza. I'm sure in time we'll understand why he doesn't want you romantically involved with Jason. Until then, you just keep trusting your instincts with that little girl and her family. I think you're probably doing a wonderful job."

That last statement gave Eliza an idea. "Glory, what if you came here to check on me? I mean, you can see first-hand how I interact with them and you could meet Jason and see what you think. I've already told Vera about you. She thinks you're an old friend that lives out of town. Which you do–if you call heaven a town."

"Actually, that's a good idea, Eliza. Then, I could report my findings directly to you know who and help you figure things out. When do you want me to come?"

"Soon. What if you happened to come back to see me because you forgot to give me my Christmas present?"

"That would work. In the next few days, maybe?"

"Today's going to be tough to get out and get you a present, but I'll make time tomorrow, so the day after? Say you come for dinner? Then, you'll get to see me in action."

Glory chuckled. "I'll keep your cooking secret. I think that's a fine time to visit."

"I can't wait for you to see the angel tree," Eliza rushed on, "and how adorable Angel is and how wonderful Vera is and…"

This time, Glory out and out laughed. "Okay, okay, I get the picture. Five o'clock the day after tomorrow. What would you like for Christmas?"

Eliza suddenly became sullen. "You can't give me what I really want for Christmas."

"Try me."

"I want to be with Jason and his family *and* see my parents again."

"Well... I'll work on it."

"Really?"

"Yes, really. Let's just take this one day at a time. See you soon. I'll surprise you with a present."

Eliza folded her cell phone and placed it on her dresser. She had hope in her heart. Maybe... just maybe... she wouldn't get her hopes up too high though, but she knew God would answer her prayer. Whether it turned out the way she wanted? Only He knew what lay ahead.

The next morning, Eliza realized Angel spent another night alone in her room the whole night through. It made her so happy the little girl adjusted so well. Now, she had to decide if she wanted to bother Vera or attempt to make breakfast herself. She figured she could scramble eggs and put bacon in the microwave. Yeah, she'd handle breakfast herself. After last night, she didn't want to see Vera overdo it. Besides, the doctor's appointment would sneak up on them.

Eliza showered, slipped on a dressy pair of pants and matching sweater and headed for the kitchen. It seemed her world revolved around food. Odd. Considering she had so little experience with it. Yes, she'd always eaten good meals wherever she worked, and she'd been a fast food fanatic, but she'd never been asked to lift a finger when it came to cooking meals.

Eliza got the surprise of her life when she entered the kitchen. Jason stood with his back to her. He had made waffles in the waffle maker. She cleared her voice, and Jason turned. She felt a warm glowing sensation all over her body.

"I thought you only made peanut butter and jelly."

He smiled. "I've been known to have a few of my own dishes down pat. Waffles happen to be one of them.

"What else can you make?" Eliza teased.

"Ham sandwiches and a wicked can of soup," he opened the waffle maker and flopped two more waffles on a plate already stacked high.

"Well that should do it. Like Belgium waffles with strawberries and whipped cream?"

"Who wouldn't?" Eliza groaned, "I swear living in this family is going to make me fat."

Without thinking, Jason said, "I have a hard time believing that since you have a perfect figure."

Eliza didn't know what to say so she just let that one slide. "How's your mother?"

"Sound asleep when I peeked in on her. After breakfast, I'm going to call the doctor and see if he can check her over this afternoon."

"I think that's a good idea. I hope everything is all right," Eliza worried her lip.

"Me too," Jason said quietly, "I guess I just thought…" he let his sentence hang.

"Jason, it's easy to believe because it seemed like a miracle that her cancer went into remission. It gave you more time, but you have to accept the fact she's living on borrowed time."

"I know. I never came to grips with that with Kathleen. She died of breast cancer. The process took a long, slow number of years, but unlike my mother, she got worse every day, never better."

"See what the doctor has to say, and treasure every moment you have together is my advice. Not that I'm being asked."

Jason turned off the waffle maker. He moved forward now at arm's length with her. Simply reach out is all he had to do… but something stopped him. He needed reassurance. He needed her advice, firmly convinced he needed her in his life, permanently. Since Kathleen's death three years prior, there had been many women who made it clear they'd like a relationship with him. Then he had his friends, like Jeff, who tried fixing him up with dates. Until Eliza, he'd never even questioned his loyalty to his deceased wife. He didn't mind being celibate. He had his work and his family, but now he had a taste of companionship which is what he had with Kathleen, but he had to admit in his heart of hearts, Eliza made him feel things Kathleen never did. It confused him and even made him feel guilty about his feelings, but try as he might, he couldn't control them. Eliza made him see and feel things differently, but she'd made it clear about their relationship; he was her employer and friend only. He had to accept that and move on. Maybe it simply meant at long last his heart healed.

"Maybe tomorrow after Angel gets out of school we can go pick up her puppy. I'll call the pound later to see if we've been approved. It'll give Angel happy moments, and I know she'd want her grandmother to see him."

"That's fine. I'd love to go. Which reminds me. You said I could invite someone over?"

Jason tensed. He didn't prepare himself to watch Eliza with a boyfriend. But…he'd offered. "Sure. Any time," he said in a clipped voice.

"I invited Glory to dinner. When she came in last time, she forgot to bring my Christmas present. So, she's coming into town tomorrow. I thought you wouldn't mind…I'll still make dinner."

"No, you won't have time if we go to the pound. How about you take the night off and we order in. My favorite restaurant has fabulous strombolies. We can get a big antipasto to go with it. Angel and Mom will love it," Jason put the plate of waffles in the middle of the table. As he gathered up the strawberries and whipped cream, he released a huge breath. *Thank God she only invited a girlfriend to dinner,* but how long would it be before he'd have to watch her with some other man?

"One more thing, Jason. Would you mind if I slipped out after breakfast for a bit. I don't have a present for Glory."

"Not a problem. Do you need me to pick up Angel from school?"

"Oh, no. I won't be that long. Besides, you'll be busy with the doctor. I'll go after you drop off Angel at school. That way, someone will be here for your mother."

"Thank you for always thinking about her."

"I'd say it's my job, but I'd feel the same way even if it wasn't."

"I know. That's what I like about you," and Jason meant it.

Angel came running into the kitchen. "How do I look?" she asked as she twirled around.

135

"Beautiful as always, Pumpkin," Jason said as he easily lifted her into his strong arms, "Did you do this by yourself, or did grandma help you?"

"Nope. I picked out my own clothes and got dressed by myself. I even brushed my teeth and my hair."

"You're getting to be such a big girl. What am I going to do when my baby is all grown up?"

"I'll always be your baby, Daddy," Angel kissed him on the cheek.

Jason deposited Angel back on the floor. "Eat up," he said.

Eliza took a seat while Jason went to check on his mother. He came back with the same news. Obviously Vera needed her sleep.

Angel chattered non stop, and if she hadn't they would have eaten in silence. Jason appeared deep in thought contemplating his feelings. He wondered why he felt so strongly for Eliza. He also worried about his reaction to her questioning whether she could invite a friend over for dinner. He felt an incredible surge of relief when he realized she didn't yet have a special man in her life.

Eliza cleaned up, and Jason took an oblivious Angel to school. Once finished, the kitchen sparkled as always. Satisfied with her work, Eliza dressed for the cold climate and made her way to the nearby mall. *What to buy Glory heaven only knew.*

Eliza pushed past throngs of people gathered to see Santa Claus. She shook her head when she found a place where she could actually stand without being elbow to elbow with people. The holiday shopping season was in full swing. Eliza looked around the mall wondering what store would have something in it that Glory would like. What would an angel who lived in heaven possibly need? Books? No. Sweater? No. Perfume? She doubted it. Eliza began walking again. Then, she spotted it. A video store. Glory used modern technology to communicate with her angels and all the angels now knew how to play DVDS. She rushed into the store knowing exactly which title she wanted. ITS A WONDERFUL LIFE. Eliza's loved it so much, she watched it every year. Instead of searching the rather large store, she approached a friendly looking cashier.

"Do you happen to have a DVD copy of IT'S A WONDERFUL LIFE?"

"Matter of fact we have a special edition for $24.99."

"I'll take it," Eliza said in response.

The cashier left his post behind the cash register and went to the back of the store. A few minutes later he returned with the movie. Eliza paid for it and decided to head home and wrap it. She only hoped Glory enjoyed it as much as she did. Once again, she battled the crowd of people swarming the mall. Once inside her car, she let out a big breath. She enjoyed shopping, but didn't like it this crazy. She hoped she and Angel wouldn't have to deal with being so crowded when she took her shopping.

Eliza unlocked the door and looked around. Not a sound. She knew Jason couldn't be home because his car didn't take up its usual spot in the driveway. She entered the kitchen and saw a note posted to the refrigerator.

TOOK MOM TO THE DOCTOR'S. WILL SEE YOU LATER.

JASON

"Well, we'll just have to wait and see," she said to nobody, but she didn't like sitting on pins and needles as she waited to hear about Vera's health. Instead of dwelling on Vera's condition, she decided to go upstairs and play her harp. It always calmed her nerves. That's how Jason and Vera found her. Upstairs playing the sweetest music Vera ever did hear.

"She's very talented," Vera said to Jason.

"Yes. At many things. You should see her ice skate. The other night, I thought she put Olympic skaters to shame."

"You've taken quite a fancy to our new friend," Vera prodded.

"She's a very special lady. She really takes good care of you and Angel."

"Not every woman would take on this family with all of its challenges," Vera tried her best to get her son to open up to her.

"You're absolutely right which is why we got lucky. Now, we're going to follow the doctor's orders and make sure you don't do more than you should."

"I'll take it easy," Vera assured her son, "I can't believe my cancer is still in remission."

"Well, let's hope it stays that way for a few more years. The doctor's right when he said that a healthy woman your age could have easily have fallen or had a weak spell. So, let's just let you listen to what your body is telling you."

"It's telling me right now that I want to go upstairs and watch that beautiful young woman play her harp."

Jason smiled, "Me, too."

Jason helped his mother up to the second floor and then knocked on Eliza's door. Suddenly, the music stopped, and Eliza opened the door. She looked from Jason to Vera and back to Jason again. She could tell by their expressions that the news couldn't be bad, so she ventured to ask Vera how she felt.

"I'm still in remission and feeling fine. I'll just have to be careful not to push myself."

Eliza impulsively hugged the older woman. "That's wonderful news!"

"Yes, my dear it is good news. Surprising, but good. How about playing me some more of that sweet music you make."

Eliza blushed. She knew Jason watched her every move, and when she'd hugged his mother, she felt an overwhelming sense of possessiveness. The kind that said this is my family.

"Although I'd love to stay around and listen to Eliza's playing, I have to go out to a site and make a bid on a job. So, I'll leave you two ladies to enjoy the afternoon. By the way, Eliza, I called the pound. They said we could pick the dog up anytime. I thought maybe the three of us could go after Angel gets out of school today."

Again. Being included in family activities. Then, when she really thought about it, Robby's family included her in some events. It's just that she felt so unsettled around Jason knowing he had feelings she shouldn't return. It just made her more aware of the fact.

"I think that sounds like fun. I'm sure Angel will be beside herself," Eliza answered.

"Good. I'll pick Angel up on the way back from my job site, so be ready to go. Mom, will you be okay for a little bit by yourself?"

"Oh, I think I'll take a nap. That way, I can oversee Eliza in the kitchen."

"By the way, we're having a dinner guest tomorrow night," Jason said not taking his eyes off Eliza.

Vera waited.

"My friend, Glory, I've been telling you about. Seems she forgot to bring me my Christmas present, and she'll be in town tomorrow night," Eliza said quietly.

Vera clapped her hands together. "That's wonderful. I can't wait to meet her."

Eliza realized Vera worried about her and it made her happy that she had a friend in this world.

"I'm off," Jason said, "If you need me, I'll have my cell phone."

The two women said goodbye. Once Eliza heard the front door close, she sat down at her harp. "Sure you're not too tired?"

"No, child. I'll let you know when I need to go to my room, but if you don't mind, I'd love to watch you play for a spell."

Eliza obliged. For one half hour she plucked on the strings of her harp. Finally, Vera had enough.

"I think it's time for that nap."

Eliza escorted Vera into her room. She fluffed her pillows and turned down the covers.

"Jason and Angel should be home soon. When you wake up, you'll find a new little furry friend in your house," Eliza smiled thinking about the beautiful Golden Retriever about to join the family.

"Yes, and don't you forget to wake me when you get back. We'll make a simple stir fry. Won't take long, and there's plenty of fresh vegetables in the refrigerator. All I need you to do is to thaw the beef sirloin tips that are in the freezer."

"Will do," she bent and kissed Vera's cheek, "Sleep well."

Eliza closed the door and returned to her room. She took out the bag with the wrapping paper and bow and her movie purchase. Scissors and tape that's what she needed. She went off in search of them. It turned out, Angel had both in her room. After carefully wrapping Glory's present. She put it in her closet with her other presents. She looked at the clock and realized she had time to wrap a few more presents.

Angel came bounding up the stairs and into Eliza's room.

"We're getting Rufus! Come on, Eliza. Let's go!" She grabbed Eliza by the hand and pulled her in the direction of the steps. Eliza just laughed at the little girl's excitement.

"So, it's Rufus is it?"

Angel stopped and asked sincerely, "Don't you like that name?"

"Oh, I think it's a fine name and very fitting for your puppy."

"Good because I wouldn't want you to not like his name."

"Honey, it doesn't matter what I think."

"Sure it does. Daddy likes the name, too."

Eliza and Angel met Jason at the bottom of the steps. Like his daughter, he wore his winter coat which was a long black cashmere coat and matching driving gloves. She hurriedly got dressed for the frigid temperatures, and the three of them went off for Rufus.

They arrived at the pound, and Angel practically danced into the shelter. Jason signed some papers and paid the sixty dollars. A young girl came out of the back room with Rufus securely on a leash. She handed it over to Angel. "Here's your puppy. Don't forget to take good care of him," the girl knelt down next to Angel, "I'm going to miss this fellow, but I'm glad he's found a good home."

"Oh, I'll take good care of Rufus," Angel promised. Rufus, full of energy, started jumping up on Angel. He licked her face, and she giggled, "Down, Rufus, down," the little girl ordered to no avail. Rufus kept licking her face and hands.

"Let's go, Sweetheart," Jason said to his daughter.

Angel gently tugged on the leash. "Come on, Rufus. Let's go home and play. I can't wait 'til grandma sees you. She'll love you."

"I'm sure she will."

The trio managed to get Rufus in the car and make their way home. The entire way, Rufus alternated between pacing back and forth and licking Angel's face.

Eliza smiled as she listened to Angel's giggles and her talking to her new pet. There was nothing sweeter than hearing a child's laughter. It brought her back to a time when Robby used to laugh and play. Unfortunately, the laughter died the sicker he got until the time came when he became even too weak to speak. She'd inquire of Glory tomorrow how Robby was doing wherever he may be.

When Jason, Eliza, Angel and Rufus entered the house they caught a whiff of something cooking. Angel ran into the kitchen, Rufus on her heels.

"Grandma, grandma, here's Rufus," Angel said as Rufus proceeded to jump up on Vera. Eliza couldn't help thinking about how big Rufus was for a puppy. She only wondered how much bigger he would get.

"Well now, Rufus, you're going to have to learn to mind your manners," Vera said patting the dog.

Rufus sniffed the air.

"Ut oh. I think Rufus is hungry," Angel said.

"Luckily, the shelter gave us some of his food and biscuits until we can get to the store and buy more supplies," Jason commented. He also pulled a squeaky toy from his coat pocket, "but, we don't have any dog bowls."

"I guess we weren't as prepared for Rufus as we should have been," Eliza noted.

Vera reached up into a cabinet and pulled out two old margarine bowls. "This will do fine for now," she proceeded to fill one with water, while Jason dumped some dry dog food into the other bowl. Angel took the food and put it in the corner of the kitchen.

"There. Now he can have his own little place. We have to get him a doggy bed, Daddy, so he can sleep in my room."

"Why do I have a feeling he's going to be sleeping in your bed?" Jason quizzed his little angel.

Angel just shrugged and smiled a secret smile.

"Just as I thought. I'm one step ahead of you, Angel Baby."

"Please, Daddy…"

Jason turned to Eliza. "What do you think about the sleeping arrangements?"

"I think they'll be just fine in one bed."

Vera nodded her approval. "You're grandfather and me had a dog when we first got married, and he always slept at the bottom of our bed. Was like a child to us," Vera said thinking back to another time and place. Eliza caught the wistful look in the older woman's eyes.

Angel released Rufus from his leash. The moment she did, he headed straight for the room with the Christmas tree.

"You're going to have to watch him, Angel, so he doesn't eat something or knock over the tree. He's your responsibility now."

"I know, Daddy. I will. Eliza will help. Right, Eliza?"

With a face so sweet, Eliza couldn't possibly say no. "Of course I will. I said I would the first day we met. Remember?"

"Yes. You're the best nanny ever," Angel impulsively threw her arms around Eliza's waist.

Eliza felt Angel's excitement and happiness, and it relieved her to have such a good feeling. She also felt Jason's unswerving feeling of possession toward her. Well, at least Angel started to think of her as a nanny and not a stepmother. Somehow, that left an empty feeling in Eliza's heart.

"Dinner's ready," Vera announced to the crowd, "Eliza, I thought I'd give you the night off. Sit. I'm feeling fine and wouldn't say so if I didn't."

Everyone sat at their place, and Rufus even plopped down next to Angel's chair looking a bit tired from his romp through the house.

"It's a vegetable stir fry tonight. I already added the soy sauce, so you shouldn't need it, but the bottle's on the table in case you need more."

Eliza watched as Jason took the huge bowl of fresh vegetables and rice and put a large portion on Angel's dish. Then, he did the same for himself and Vera. When done doing that, he passed the bowl to Eliza.

Eliza scooped up a sizeable amount and placed it on her plate. She quickly tasted the fare and immediately complimented Vera on such a tasty dish. "You'll have to teach me how to make this one, too," she said to a knowing Vera.

"Of course, my dear. You'll learn all my recipes."

"You know, I'm going to have two nights off from cooking. I can't wait until you meet Glory. You're all going to like her very much. She's very sweet."

"Any friends of yours are always welcome in our house," Vera smiled, "It'll do you good to be with your friend.

"I bought her a DVD copy of IT'S A WONDERFUL LIFE," Eliza announced to the group.

"That's one of my favorite movies," Jason stated. Vera seconded the opinion.

"Did I ever see that movie, Daddy?" Angel inquired.

"Honey, I don't recall you ever seeing it. We'll have to get our own copy. I'm sure you'd like it very much. It's a story about an angel getting his wings."

Angel perked right up.

"He has an assignment. He has to help a human on earth before he can become a full fledged angel."

"Kinda like you, Eliza. You're helping us. Maybe you'll get angel wings someday."

Eliza almost choked on her carrot. Angel didn't realize how close to the truth she'd come.

At that moment, Rufus decided to jump up and lick some rice off of Angel's plate.

"Bad doggie," Angel reprimanded Rufus, "You have your own food over there," she said pointing to his dish.

Rufus meekly laid at her feet as though he understood what Angel was saying.

"That's interesting," Jason observed, "Maybe, he's been trained to understand bad and good dog. After all, he's almost one year old."

"We'll know for sure when he has to do his business," Eliza laughed.

"You'd better not decide to do your duty on our rug," Vera said wagging her finger at the dog with the big brown eyes. Eliza now knew where the saying *puppy dog eyes* came from.

After dinner, Jason said he would work for a little while and then meet Vera, Eliza, Angel and Rufus in the tree room. Before Jason could retreat to his office, Eliza caught him on the steps.

"When you get a chance, I'd like to talk to you about something."

"Why don't you come up to my office now?" Jason wondered what

Eliza needed to talk to him about. He hoped she wouldn't be leaving...that he hadn't scared her off.

"Give me a minute, and I'll meet you upstairs. I just want to let Vera and Angel know where I'll be."

"Okay," Jason continued to climb the stairs as Eliza informed the two persons in her life that had become her family that she had to talk to Jason. A few minutes later, she stood in Jason's immaculate office. Seated behind the desk, he somehow didn't look intimidating like some men did when they were in the role of business man.

"What can I do for you?" he probed.

"Jason, I had an idea I wanted to run by you. I talked to Vera about this, but I really would like to hear your thoughts on my idea."

"I'd be happy to listen," Jason leaned forward all ears.

"Well, I just thought, since Vera has such wonderful down home recipes, you would consider opening a diner. You could hire someone to follow her recipes and call it Vera's Place."

There. She had put it out there. If he thought her crazy, he didn't show it. Instead, he leaned back in his chair. "I think that is a wonderful idea. Kind of like a tribute to my mother. Of course, I don't have time to run a diner, but I certainly could back one if I found a partner who could."

"Maybe you could just place an ad in the paper and interview prospects," Eliza suggested, excited at the possibilities, "I'd be happy to help out when needed.

"Let me mull it over, and I'll get back to you."

"Thank you," and Eliza rose to go back downstairs.

"Eliza..."

She turned.

"No, thank *you*. It's a wonderful idea. Let me just see if I can swing it."

Eliza realized she hadn't considered the capitol needed to start up such a business this made her move into private areas of Jason's life. She nodded.

"Would you like to go to a movie with Angel and me some Saturday evening? There's a good Christmas movie playing at the Center Theater."

Eliza felt it again. This time the feeling overwhelmed her and pulled her toward him. She looked at him and felt it, a powerful surge of protection.

Eliza answered the only way she knew how. From her heart. "I'd love to."

Jason smiled, and she felt his joy at her response.

"Did you plan on taking Angel to get her picture taken with Santa Claus?"

"Yeah. I planned on it. I just don't know when. Maybe we can go before the movie."

"That's a good idea considering the Center Theater is right across the street from the mall, but I warn you, it's a battleground there."

Jason laughed. "I'm taking it, it's been pretty hectic shopping for your Christmas presents?"

"To say the least."

"Well I won't ask you to come with me then," he rose from his chair.

"Where?" he had Eliza curious.

"To help me play Santa Claus to Angel."

Before she could stop herself, the words were out of her mouth. "But, I'd love to help you pick out presents."

Jason's smile faded. "Then, let's make it a date," playing Santa Claus made what they were about to do serious and not exactly your typical date. Then again, Eliza couldn't be considered your typical woman.

Even though Eliza understood perfectly what Jason suggested, she decided to ignore it and pretend he meant date as in the same kind of date she had with Glory tomorrow night.

She smiled. "It's a date."

Jason moved closer. Eliza didn't move. She knew he wanted to hold her. Since the night of their shared kiss, he hadn't attempted any physical contact. For that matter, he hadn't acted anything but the part of employer and friend. One step forward, and she'd be in his arms. It took all her strength to turn and leave him wondering why she fought her feelings so hard.

Once in the safety of the stairwell, Eliza closed her eyes and breathed. It seemed difficult to remember that simple task when in Jason's presence.

"*Okay, you know who. Why are you doing this to me? To test me? To make me miserable because I can't have the two things I want most? I've served you well for many years. I've always given you my all...my heart...my soul has always recognized you as my God and I the humble servant, but I'm having a hard time right now. How can I stay here with him when I want him to make love to me? I've never been made love to, yet I know it's what I need with him. It's like I've always known him... his soul and mine go way back, I think. I'm rambling. I'm sorry, dear God. Please guide me and make it easier on me. All I ask is that I do what I came here to do rather quickly and move on to my next assignment. Amen. Ooooh! I don't ask that you rush Vera's passing just my finding a woman capable of completing my task and loving Jason and Angel the same way I do. Amen again.*"

Eliza composed herself and walked into the room she considered the most beautiful in the whole house. The one with the tree that emanated the love of a woman who had loved the man and child she had come to love too.

CHAPTER FOURTEEN

"Are you all right, dear?" Vera asked. She sat on the couch with Angel, Rufus laying between them.

"Fine. I see couches are okay, too," she said changing the subject.

"Rufus won't hurt anything, Eliza," Angel hugged her new dog, "We'll make sure he's a good puppy."

"Yes, well what shall we do tonight?"

"Jason said he'd be down shortly. Maybe he'll think of something," Vera replied. She looked a little tired, but not so that she should go to bed unless she wanted.

"Actually, I'm not feeling so good and wondered if you wouldn't mind telling Jason that I retired early. Perhaps Angel can go one night without a bath."

"I knew something was wrong the minute you walked in here," Vera tsk'd her, "You leave me with my grandbaby, and I'll make sure Jason knows you're not well. If you don't feel good in the morning, I expect you to sleep in. I'll have no problem making breakfast for my family. I'll just turn in earlier than expected."

Eliza walked over to Vera and took her two hands in her own. "How can I thank you for always being so kind?"

"Love my family, Eliza, and you love me," a wise woman, Vera recognized the signs of love. She knew Eliza fought her feelings for her son, but she didn't understand why a woman alone in the world would turn her back on love from a man who would make her happy.

"Goodnight," Eliza kissed both Angel and Vera on the cheek, "and goodnight to you, too," she patted Rufus's head, and the dog wagged its tail.

"I think he's starting to recognize his name, Eliza. I called him before and he came running. He jumped up on the couch next to me and grandma."

"I think it's a bit soon for Rufus to respond to his name, but he will soon enough. He probably just wanted to do what you were doing."

"Oh," Angel sounded dejected.

"We'll have to train him. In fact, before I go to bed, I'll take him outside."

Eliza retrieved her coat and gloves from the closet. She ducked into the kitchen and grabbed Rufus's leash. "Here we go, Rufus. Do you have to go out?" she talked gently to the dog as she put on his leash, "Come on, Rufus, let's go out."

The dog followed obediently. Five minutes later Eliza came back into the house with a smile on her face. "I think Rufus is trained to go out. Maybe I'm wrong, but I don't think so. He seemed to know exactly what to do. He should be fine through the night, Angel."

"Thank you, Eliza. I know you don't feel good. I'll take care of him now and you go to bed." Angel sounded like a little old lady. She took hold of Rufus's leash and unhooked him. The dog ran into the living room and jumped back up on the couch.

"Wait until he gets to sleep in your bed. He may never come down he'll be so comfy," Eliza said ruffling Angel's hair. She hung up her coat and made her way back up the stairs to the sanctity of her room. A beautiful room. She remembered how concerned Jason was at first that she wouldn't like it. He always seemed concerned about her well being. She could define her feelings right now. Lonely. She couldn't have Jason and Angel. She couldn't yet have her Mom and Dad. She had Glory and a ray of hope that Glory could intercede for her. She should be grateful.

As she changed into her flannel nightgown, she said a quick prayer blessing all those she loved through the years. That included Jason and his family. She sunk into the bed and pulled the down comforter up to her neck. It felt good not to worry. Right now, the only thing she could think about was what Vera said about tomorrow morning. She could sleep in. She didn't know yet if she'd be ready to face Jason again. Though she hoped he'd follow through on her idea should he have the funding. Soon sleep claimed her, and she had a dream.

She played in a meadow with children. She laughed as they chased her. Everyone, including herself, had bare feet. Then Rufus appeared. She stopped to pet the dog, and the moment she touched him she knew. He'd been housebroken by beatings. The man who trained him hit him mercilessly, and dropped him off on the side of the highway late one night when he got sick of him. Rufus had traveled miles of highway whimpering as the cars came at him with their bright lights. More than once, he almost got hit. Relief for him came when an old lady pulled over to the side of the road and opened her door. This lady had taken him to the pound hoping he'd find a good family. The girl at the pound had been mistaken. Rufus didn't cause any allergies. With that the dream faded. Someone wanted her to know Rufus's history. She also knew that Rufus missed his mother and father and brothers and sisters. He had feelings and needs just like people. Then again, Eliza knew animals had amazing instincts as did all God's creatures. Now she'd become attached to Rufus as well. Just something else she loved and had to leave behind. Somehow, all of this registered in her sleep.

The next morning sunlight streaming in through the stained glass window woke Eliza. She sat up and looked at the clock. Ten a.m. Wow, she really had slept in and it made her grateful that Vera promised to make breakfast for Jason and Angel. She'd purposely not set her alarm. She figured if she woke at her usual time, she'd do her job. If she'd didn't, she'd take Vera up on her offer. The latter won out. Slowly, she climbed out of bed and rummaged through her closet. What to wear? Glory would be there for dinner, so she wanted to look nice, but comfortable. She settled on a black turtle neck, a black and white houndstooth skirt that hit just above the knee, black stockings and low-heeled pumps to match. She added a strand of white pearls around her neck and dangling pearl earrings. Then, she proceeded to pile her long hair up on top of her head. She looked in the mirror, pleased with her appearance. She looked like she worked in an office not a home. She hadn't showered because she really didn't feel up to it. She quickly fixed her make-up and headed downstairs. Rufus greeted her at the bottom of the steps.

"Do you have to go out boy?" Eliza stressed the word out so he'd start connecting it with going outside.

"He's already been out twice this morning. Seems our friend here has been well trained. He barked at the front door first thing this morning, then again after breakfast."

Jason had come up behind her. It unnerved Eliza that she hadn't felt his presence like she always did. Could she be becoming desensitized? She remembered her dream and looked down at the dog that patiently sat by her feet, tail wagging, waiting for her to pet him. She bent down.

"You poor thing. No one here will ever hurt you," she whispered so that only the dog could hear. As though he understood what she said, he thumped his tail harder.

"Well," she stood, "I guess I needed my rest."

"Mom told me you didn't feel well. How are you doing this morning?"

"Much better, and I'm glad because Glory will be here tonight. In fact, I'm going back up to get her present so that I can put it underneath the Christmas tree before I forget," she ran up the stairs and out of sight before Jason could respond. She'd do anything so that she didn't have to be alone with him.

Eliza opened the closet door and took out the small present. She admired the wrapping paper and congratulated herself on a job well done. The leaves with holly berries tucked behind the small ribbon made the package all the more festive. She took a deep breath and realized she couldn't hide from Jason forever. She just had to face him and know, no matter if a future with him and Angel affected her not seeing her parents again. She did want to see them at least once more. She desperately longed for them, the same way she longed for Jason's arms around her. She'd had a small taste of what that heaven on earth could be like.

A quick trip down the stairs brought her into the tree room. She gently placed Glory's present beneath it and noticed a small box with her name on it. It read from Jason. So, he'd bought her a present. She thought maybe him being her employer he'd just give her a holiday bonus. Nope. He'd gone personal, and so had she. Rufus's barking brought her back to reality. It sounded like the barking came from the kitchen. She hoped not alone. She ventured in only to find Jason at the table reading the morning newspaper and Vera fussing over the stove making it shine. Rufus lay on a cushion in the corner.

"That makes a good dog bed," she said hoping her voice didn't waver.

Jason put down the paper. "It's from an old couch we stored in the attic. It'll have to do until I can get out and pick him up a proper dog bed. In fact, the stores are all open now. I think I'll run to the pet store and pick up more food and supplies."

He quickly left the room. Seconds later, Eliza heard the door close.

"How are you feeling, dear?" Vera sat at the head of the table and motioned for her to sit along side of her.

"Much better. Thanks for taking over this morning."

"Think nothing of it."

"Which brings me to how are you feeling?"

"Like my old self, and it feels good. When I said my prayers last night, I explained to Henry that my work on earth had yet to be done. That God kept me here for some reason I couldn't know. I think he understood. Does that sound strange?"

Eliza thought about it for a moment. "No, I think those we love can hear our prayers or know when we're coming to join them or not."

"Well, I happen to think I'm still with my two feet on this earth because I have to see Jason and Angel settled into a new life without me. Just an old lady's opinion."

"Maybe. Or, maybe you're here to help me."

"How can I help you, Eliza?"

"By telling me that your son doesn't have feelings for me."

Vera raised her eyebrows, surprised by the admission. "I can't do that, Child, because I know, as only a mother knows, that he does. The question is do you return those feelings?"

"I can't Vera. I have a good reason why, and you'll just have to trust that. I'm here to help you and to help Jason find another wife and mother for Angel."

"What makes you think that?"

"Just a feeling," Eliza realized she'd said too much.

"Well, I can't imagine why you wouldn't want to be with my son and grandchild when it's obvious you care so much about them. I'm not blind you know. As for you finding him a wife, you already have. You just have to admit to yourself it's you."

"You're a wise old woman, Vera. I already have come to terms with my decision to stay Jason's employee and friend. You should too. You can help me encourage Jason to find another woman to spend his life with."

"Pish. You do what you have to do, and I'll do what I have to do."

Eliza rose. When Vera made up her mind about something it seemed nothing stopped her. "Would you like some coffee?"

"Tea for me, dear."

Eliza filled the kettle and placed it on the stove. She turned the burner up to high. Once the coffee perked, she returned to the table determined not to talk about her feelings with Vera.

"I'm all caught up with the cleaning, so I think I'll spend some time in my room playing my harp. Would you like to join me?"

"Yes, as a matter of fact I would. Perhaps, you can read to me again from that angel book of yours."

Eliza smiled. "This family has a thing for angels."

"I find them fascinating. I also happen to agree with Angel. I think you're going to get your wings."

Eliza laughed. "Vera, you'll be the first to know if I do, but I have a feeling I won't be getting them until I've gone to cooking school."

"What do you think we've been doing?" Vera asked.

"We've been pretending your cooking is mine."

"So we have. Well how about we plan to make a dessert for tonight after we're done playing and reading? You'll do it all by yourself. I'll just tell you what to do."

"Sounds like a good way to spend the afternoon. Come on, let's go up to my room," Eliza stood and reached for Vera's elbow. She helped her up, and then put her arm around her waist.

"You come too, Rufus," Eliza addressed the dog, "We can't leave you down here by yourself where you can get into trouble."

As though the dog understood every word, he slowly stretched and trotted up the steps behind them. Once in Eliza's room, he plopped down in a corner. The next few hours were spent with Eliza entertaining Vera with her harp and then her reading. Before she knew it, the time to pick Angel up from school came. She didn't know if Jason returned or not because the music drowned out all other sounds in the house like the squeaking floorboards on certain steps.

"I'll be back with Angel, and we can start my first cooking lesson. By the way, do you have all of your recipes written down somewhere?"

Vera tapped the side of her head. "They're all up here."

"Would you mind, when you get time, writing them all down for me?"

"Time I have. I'll start on it now. Did you leave my notebook in my room?"

"It's on your dresser. I'd really like it if you could do as many recipes as you can, for all kinds of things."

"I'll get them all down. Might take me a week or two, but it's a project worth working on."

"Thanks, Vera," Eliza slipped out the door and down the long staircase. No sign of Jason. Rufus had stayed with Vera in her room, so she knew he wouldn't be knocking down the Christmas trees or eating any angel ornaments, though something told her he wouldn't anyway. So far, he'd proved to them he was fully trained. Eliza remembered her dream again. Glory always told her God talked to people through their dreams sometimes. She knew for certain Vera's dream about her husband proved to her to be one such case and doubly certain in Rufus's case. He needed to be handled with TLC because he'd had a hard life since being a young pup. Eliza had a soft spot in her heart for animals and children. Robby had wanted a dog, but his parents thought an animal would get too attached to him. They had fully accepted the fact that their loved one had an early death in his cards. Very few families she worked with over the years thought like that.

Eliza stood in her usual spot, and as usual, Bill Wiggins approached her. She admitted him to be a handsome man. Tall, well built and always with a smile on his face. She'd learned he had a genuinely happy-go-lucky attitude most of the time, but he didn't even come close to Jason.

"Howdy, Eliza. How are you doing today? You sure look lovely."

By now, Eliza accepted his flattering comments. The next comment took her by surprise.

"You know how you mentioned that time we should get the girls together for a play date?"

Eliza nodded now knowing what he would ask next.

"What do you say you bring Angel over to my house this afternoon. They can play for awhile, and I'll even make dinner for us. I make a mean spaghetti sauce."

Relieved that she had a genuine excuse, Eliza replied, "I'm sorry, Bill. I'd love to, but an old friend from out of town is coming to dinner tonight. Another time, maybe?"

Bill smiled. "Sure. You just say when," he wanted a firm set date, and Eliza realized she had to concede.

"How about I check our schedule for next week some time? I'll let you know on Monday."

Now, Bill really smiled. He hadn't expected Eliza to come around so quickly. Thankfully, Angel and Bill's daughter interrupted their conversation with their sudden appearance. Eliza politely said goodbye. She'd have no choice but to go to Bill's house sometime next week. And after all, Angel and his daughter played together. It wouldn't be fair for her to miss out on a play date because of her. She'd just have to subtly allude to the fact a man in her life made her unavailable. No need for him to know that man didn't even know how she *really* felt about him. No. Jason had no reason to believe that she had fallen in love with him. Angel's question broke Eliza's train of thought.

"How's Rufus? Did he be a good dog all day?"

Eliza looked in her rearview mirror. "Angel, honey, please buckle your seatbelt."

Angel obliged. "Well?"

"He's very obedient. I also know he missed you very much."

"Soon as I get home I'm going to change my clothes so I can play with Rufus until dinner time. Daddy said we're having strombolies tonight."

"Yes, and we'll have a special dinner guest."

Angel was all ears.

"My friend Glory is in town and wanted to drop by for a visit and to exchange Christmas presents since I won't see her for a while."

"That's the one you bought the DVD for, right?"

"Ah ha. I'm betting your going to like her."

"Daddy told me I had to be on my best behavior tonight."

"You're always good, Angel Baby."

"Maybe I should wear something nicer than my play clothes?" A typical question from Angel.

"That's a good idea. Nothing too dressy though since you'll be romping around the house with Rufus."

Eliza expertly pulled into her spot in front of Jason's house. Angel got out the door like a shot. By the time Eliza caught up with her, Angel laughed and hugged her new pet. Rufus, it seemed, had been lonely.

"Would you like help picking out something to wear?"

"No. I can do that by myself, but I would like it if you'd put my hair in a pony tail with a bow."

"Bring your hair supplies down to the kitchen once you're dressed."

Angel went running up the steps.

Eliza noted Jason's car sat in its usual spot in the driveway so she knew the inevitable would happen. She'd have to face him. She just didn't know if that meant now or later. So, she carefully walked into the kitchen hoping to find him. She'd missed him today. Instead, Vera greeted her. "I have everything you need to make chocolate fudge brownies right here on the counter."

"Let me put on an apron, and I'll be right with you."

Eliza walked over to the other side of the kitchen where there were rows of drawers. She pulled out a full piece apron and slipped it over her head and tied it around her small waist. That's when she noticed the new plaid dog bed in the corner. It clashed horribly with the kitchen's colors. She also saw a large red container that had a sticker that read "Dog Food." Along side of it, sat a few more dog toys.

"I guess Jason did quite a bit of shopping for Rufus," Eliza commented.

Vera just shrugged. "It's about time he gave into my little girl's wishes. He held off on getting her a dog until you came along. It's not like she has any brothers or sisters to play with."

"I sensed there was something there between them at my interview."

"Angel would plead with her father, and he would always say some day. Thank goodness someday has arrived. Said he had fun looking at all the puppies for sale. He even talked about getting a kitten for Angel. Thought he might put it under the Christmas tree."

Eliza smiled. "I just hope Rufus will get along with a kitten," she could just imagine the oversized puppy chasing a speck of a kitten around.

"They say it's best to introduce them when they're young. I'm sure things will work out. You do know that means more work for you?"

"If it makes Angel happy, I don't mind. Now what do I do first?"

CHAPTER FIFTEEN

The doorbell rang precisely at five o'clock. Eliza smoothed the front of her skirt and opened the door. Glory stood on the other side wearing a conservative navy blue pea coat and pants to match. Impulsively, she threw her arms around Glory.

"I'm so glad you could make it," she said ushering her friend and supervisor through the door. "Here, let me take your coat."

Glory looked around the foyer and then up the cherry wood staircase. "It's a beautiful house."

"Jason designed it himself. Modern Victorian. I think that's what he calls it."

"You must be Glory," Jason came up behind Eliza and extended his hand in greeting. Once again, Eliza failed to feel his presence. She wondered why.

Glory took the offered hand and smiled. "I've heard so much about you and your family. Thank you for inviting me to dinner."

"It's our pleasure. Any friend of Eliza's is a friend of ours."

Glory had to admit, *knock down dead out and out right gorgeous didn't even begin to describe Jason. No wonder her charge fought such a difficult battle. If his manners and personality turned out anything like his looks, he'd be dam near perfect.* She didn't get the chance to compliment Jason on the design of his home because Angel came running down the stairs in one of her matching sweatshirts. Her blonde curls hung loosely down her back in a ponytail topped off with a matching bow. Rufus at her heels.

"You must be Angel," Glory directed her comment at the little girl.

"You must be Eliza's friend, Glory. It's nice to meet you."

Glory could understand why Eliza had such a difficult time wrestling with her conscience. The little girl looked adorable.

"Hope you like stomboli because we have steak and cheese with fried onions and ham and pepperoni and cheese and sauce. Jason ordered in from his favorite restaurant so I wouldn't have to cook tonight."

Glory just smiled knowing Eliza's secret. "I don't know that I've ever had one, but I'm willing to try it."

"Oh, you'll love them. They're delicious," Angel added her two cents. Eliza noted how closely Angel watched her interaction with her friend.

"Here," Glory held out a big box wrapped in red foil with a green bow on top. I'm hoping you'll open it tonight while I'm here."

"I will. Yours is under the tree. Come on with me while I put this with it."

Together, the two angels entered the room with the enormous tree.

"Oh my," said Glory, "It certainly is something. It is beautiful. I absolutely love all the angel ornaments."

"My Mommy picked them all out for me because she said I was her angel. That's why I'm called Angel," Angel had followed the two women into the room with all her toys.

"Well, she must have loved you very much. It shows on this tree."

"She's in heaven with the angels," Angel addressed Glory.

Glory bent down. "I know. Eliza told me. You must miss her a lot."

"I don't remember her very much, but I miss having a Mommy."

Glory didn't know what to say. She started to see Eliza's dilemma.

"Time to eat," Vera's voice sounded from the kitchen. Eliza led the way. Glory noted the lack of any formal dining room. When she walked into the designer kitchen, she could see why. It had everything a formal dining room had and then some. The spectacular design spoke of a true creative talent.

Vera walked over to Glory and took her hand in her own. "It's so nice to finally meet you," she said, "I'm Vera. Jason's my son and Angel's my grandbaby."

"I feel like I know all of you. Eliza has told me so much about you."

"Make yourself at home and grab a seat."

Glory took the one closest, and Eliza sat next to her. Meanwhile, Jason and Vera took up their usual places and Angel led Rufus to his dog bed.

"He's a beautiful dog," again, Glory addressed Angel, "What kind is he?"

"He's a Golden Retriever. He's big, but the girl at the pound said he's still a puppy."

"My he's going to be big Jason," Glory turned to Eliza's employer, "I hear you're a contractor. Did you build this house?"

"Let's just say I designed it and then oversaw the construction."

"It's absolutely incredible. I'd love to see the whole house if I'm not being too rude."

Jason flushed with pride. "I'd be happy to give you a tour after dinner."

Vera already had all the stromboli's sliced and on big platters. The antipasto sat in a large ceramic bowl, and bottles of soda lined up in the center of the table. "Help yourself, Glory."

Glory selected the steak and cheese stromboli. She'd never tasted something so good. Nice to come down from heaven and be a human angel from time to time. "It's fabulous," not shy, she grabbed the thongs and helped herself to some antipasto and topped it off with Italian dressing. Eliza did the same. The group chatted amicably about the weather and Glory's background which she entirely made up. Eliza hoped she'd remember everything.

"So you supervise at a non-profit organization?" Vera asked, "Eliza didn't mention that."

"I don't think we talked too much about her. We don't get to see each other very often. We're usually busy doing different things in different places," Eliza twisted her napkin on her lap. She spoke true words. Heaven could be considered not-for-profit.

"It's good to see Eliza's not alone in this world what with her parents passing when only a child."

"She has us now," Angel added. She'd been unusually quiet during dinner. Eliza's radar kicked in and it told her Angel took in everything about Glory and made sure Glory was good enough to be her friend.

"I'm stuffed. What wonderful food. Thank you, Jason, Vera," Glory nodded in their direction.

"You better have left room for dessert. I made it all by myself," Eliza winked at Glory. She got up and retrieved a tray lined with paper lace doilies and chocolate fudge brownies with powder sugar sprinkled on top. "Try one," Eliza said as she held out the tray to her supervisor. Glory hoped Vera had made the dessert knowing what she knew about Eliza's cooking skills, or lack thereof.

Glory selected a healthy sized one and took one bite before proclaiming them delightful. Eliza passed the tray around to the others. Vera just nibbled on hers, proud of Eliza. She'd actually done a good job. Yes, she'd learn to be a good cook with time, but she didn't doubt her feelings of her already being a good candidate for her son, cooking skills or not.

"Eliza, why don't you and Glory visit in the living room. I'll clean up and put some coffee on."

Just as Eliza went to protest, Glory grabbed hold of her hand and said, "I can't wait for you to open your present."

The two beautiful women sat down on the couch and exchanged presents.

"I hope you like the movie as much as I do. It's about an angel getting his wings."

"Oh, something tells me I'll like it. Thank you," she leaned over and hugged Eliza, "Now, open yours."

Eliza managed to balance the large box on her lap. "It's a shame to rip open this paper it's so pretty," she did so anyway just like a child at Christmas. She opened the box and inside sat a large red wicker basket. She pulled the basket from the box and had to chuckle. It included a gourmet food basket with all the fixings for an Italian spaghetti dinner. It came packed with imported pasta and olive oil and a red sauce and Italian cookies.

"And all you have to do is boil water and heat the sauce," Glory smiled as she said it.

"I'm sure this will come in handy some night when I'm not up to cooking my usual extraordinary dinners."

"Hmmm," Glory looked around the room to make sure Angel hadn't followed them in, "He's quite the specimen."

"Now do you understand why I want God to let me have both things?"

"Angel's a darling. Vera's a kind old lady, and Jason is a lady killer without the killer instincts."

Eliza cocked her head.

"He only had eyes for you at dinner tonight. I'd say he's ready to move on."

"I know. I have to let go, but it so hard imagining him with another woman, Never mind handpicking her."

"I'd say you're doing a wonderful job on this assignment. Just stay the course would be my advice."

"I will. How's Robby?"

"Funny you should ask. He just asked about you. He's an angel in training much like you at his age."

"That's good to hear. You know, that he's no longer suffering. I miss him, too."

"Maybe our boss will let us have a big reunion one day."

Eliza's face lit up. "That would be wonderful. Do you really think it's a possibility?"

"Anything is possible with God, Eliza. Always remember that," at that moment, Jason entered the room holding two steaming cups of coffee, "I hope you like a little cream and sugar," he addressed Glory.

"That's fine, thank you," Glory said taking the mug from the man who held her angel's heart.

"We'll be in to join you in a few minutes," Jason ducked back into the kitchen.

The night passed quickly and at eight o'clock, Glory announced that she had to leave. She had a long ride home. Eliza walked her to the door and gave her a hug after she'd shrugged into her navy jacket. "We'll talk soon," Glory assured Eliza.

"I appreciate your coming. It meant a lot to me–your seeing him and his family first hand." Glory nodded, walked out the door and disappeared into thin air. Eliza just sighed. Time to give one sleepy little girl a quick bath.

"I liked her," a solemn Angel told Eliza, "She's pretty."

"Yes, she is Angel Baby, and she's a good friend."

"Do you think we can go over to my friend Samantha Wiggins house some day after school? She asked me over."

Eliza wondered if Bill Wiggins put his daughter up to it. "As a matter of fact, me and her Daddy are planning to get together some day next week."

"Don't forget Monday after school you're taking me Christmas shopping, so we can't go then."

"I didn't forget," Eliza said tweaking Angel's nose, "Did you break open your piggy bank?"

"I don't have to. It has a lid on the bottom you just open up. That way I don't have to buy another one."

"Do you know what you want to buy your Dad and Grandmother?"

"I'll have to look around."

"I think the dollar store has lots of nice things, and I'm betting you'll have enough money to buy them a couple of presents."

"Really?"

"Really. Now hop out and let's get you to bed so your Dad can read you a story."

"Eliza…"

"Yes, honey?"

"I had another dream last night."

That alerted Eliza immediately. She didn't sense any fear. Instead, she felt a calmness emanating from Angel. The same feeling she had picked up from her father.

"Do you want to tell me about it?"

"I dreamed that my Mommy came to visit me."

Eliza waited.

"She said you should be my new step Mommy and that it was all right with her. She told me you were a good soul. She also told me to be extra nice to Rufus because someone hurt him when he was little."

Eliza didn't know what to say. How did you explain to a six-year-old that you couldn't be her step mother no matter how badly you wanted to be, and what on earth about Rufus? Could Angel's mother really have communicated with her daughter from the other side? How else would she know about Rufus? Did that mean anything about a possible destiny with Jason? She *felt* like that sometimes. She shook her head. No. Just wishful thinking she told herself.

"Angel, to be your step Mommy means I would have to marry your Daddy."

"Daddy likes you. Grandma does too. She told me you make a fine pair."

That Vera. If Eliza didn't love the old woman so much, she'd sock her in the nose for giving her Granddaughter false hopes.

"Your Daddy and I are just friends, and I work for him. That means we're not getting married," Eliza explained, "I know you need a Mommy. One day, your Daddy will find someone he wants to marry."

"Daddy doesn't cry anymore at night. Not since you moved in."

"Now, how would you know that young lady?"

Angel slipped her nightgown over her head. She shrugged her shoulders. "Sometimes, I check on him in the night."

Eliza couldn't help thinking how grown-up Angel could be for her age. She'd been through a lot... seen a lot and had to deal with a lot of hurt and pain from a young age. "I don't think that has anything to do with me, Angel. I think your Daddy is healing. Do you know what that means?"

"To get better like when you have a cut?"

"Something like that. It means he's accepting the fact that your Mommy is in heaven and that he'll see her again one day–just not right away," Eliza was quick to add.

"Mommy told me not to be afraid of Daddy dying. She said he's not going to die for a long time 'cause he has work to do here on earth. She said her work was done that's why she's in heaven."

Eliza wondered about this dream. For a six-year-old, she spouted out a lot of spiritual things Eliza came to know only by becoming an angel.

"I believe that, sweetie."

"Then why don't you believe her when she says your going to be my step Mommy."

"Maybe she said step *nanny*."

Angel shook her head and her blonde curls bounced side to side. "Nope. I'm positive she said Mommy. You'll see."

Eliza didn't know how to explain to Angel that couldn't be possible, so as she so often did with Vera, she changed the subject. "Time for bed. Last one upstairs is a rotten egg."

Angel giggled and immediately ran off. Eliza waited a minute or two before following. When she arrived at Angel's room, the little girl that had stolen her heart already laid in bed. Jason stood in the doorway.

"Guess you win, Angel Baby," Eliza said huffing and puffing as though out of breath. She noticed the big golden dog at the bottom of the bed. "I see Rufus has adjusted well to his new home."

"He's a good dog," Jason spoke. He squared off with Eliza face to face. She felt wave after wave of love and acceptance. "Eliza, do you feel like seeing a movie tomorrow night? Like we talked about?" he sounded unsure of himself. Eliza immediately picked up on it and put him at ease.

"I think it would be so much fun. I haven't seen A MIRACLE ON 34TH STREET since... well, it's been a long time."

164

"I take it that's a yes?"

"Absolutely. There's no place I'd rather be than with you and Angel," she stared into brown eyes and understood why people said they were windows to the soul. She'd made Jason a very happy man.

"Goody. Can we go to dinner first, Daddy?"

"That's a good idea. We could eat in the Mall's Food Court and catch the seven o'clock movie."

It took all of Eliza's strength to say it, but she did. "Goodnight. I'll check in on your mother before I turn in for the night."

"Wait," Jason touched her arm, "I'd like to talk to you a few minutes about what we discussed the other day. Do you think you can meet me in my office tomorrow afternoon? I'll be at a site all morning."

"Sure. Does that mean you'll need to eat breakfast earlier than usual?"

"I'm leaving at five, so I'll just grab some coffee and donuts at the donut shop."

"Okay, see you tomorrow afternoon," Eliza slowly made her way to her room. Between father and daughter, Eliza felt exhausted by deciphering their feelings toward her. Both wanted her. One for a life partner. The other for a mother. She closed her door and leaned against it. *Pulling off this assignment...definitely not going to be easy.*

CHAPTER SIXTEEN

Eliza woke up Saturday morning half an hour earlier than usual. She decided to forgo her shower because she had some heavy duty cleaning to tend to. She slipped on her sweat suit and sneakers and proceeded across the hall to check on Vera—not in her bedroom.

Eliza quietly descended the long, winding staircase so as not to wake Angel. She reached the kitchen and found Vera sitting at the kitchen table, a cup of coffee in front of her. She stared off into space. She jumped at Eliza's arrival.

"I'm sorry, I didn't mean to sneak up on you," Eliza said, "You're up early."

"Couldn't sleep. I had another dream about Henry."

Eliza felt with every bone in her body that this dream could be significant and had greatly affected Vera.

"He came to tell me my time is coming, and I have to accept the fact I might not see Jason married off again."

Eliza felt a surge of despair coming from the older woman. "Vera, Jason has had a tough three years, he's shown no interest in women, so I don't think it's realistic to believe he's going to marry sometime in the near future. You have to accept it. I think Henry is just trying to prepare you…make you accept the truth," Eliza covered Vera's freehand with her own.

"Child, I see how my son looks at you. I see how more involved he is with Angel. The three of you act like family."

"That's my job, Vera. To take care of Jason and you and Angel. Jason's not going to propose to me tomorrow, and I'm not going to marry him. Please realize that. I don't want you passing thinking I don't care for your son. I do. Very much, but I'm being a realist here."

Vera heaved a heavy sigh. "I guess Henry might be right. You're stubborn. You refuse to see what's right under your nose."

"How about we call a truce?"

Vera gave her an odd look. "We're not fighting."

"No, we're not fighting, but there's been this tug of war between us, you pushing me and Jason together and me backing off. How about I make you a promise I can keep."

Vera took a sip of her now lukewarm coffee. "Go on."

"I promise to take the best care that I possibly can of Jason and Angel. I promise I'll be sure to guide him in the right direction when a woman he wants to marry comes along, and I'll stay with them until they're settled as a family."

"Then what will you do?"

Eliza smiled a sad smile. "Do as I always do. Move on to the next people who need me."

"Why don't you want to get involved with anyone? I would think a young thing like you, beautiful and all, would have many men chasing after you. Yet, you choose a solitary life. I just don't comprehend that."

"If it makes you feel better, I have a date lined up for next week."

Vera perked right up.

"He's the father of one of Angel's friends. We're setting up a playdate for next week, and he's going to make us a spaghetti dinner."

"Hmmm. Does Jason know this?"

"I didn't think he would mind. After all, it is one of Angel's good friends from school."

"I don't mean about taking Angel. I mean about your dinner date?"

Eliza squirmed in her seat. "No. I had no reason to tell him, yet. I will mention it because I'm taking Angel with me."

"I think that's a good idea. Enough talk. I've made some buttermilk pancakes. I got up early because I knew Jason had to be out of the house at five."

"Vera, I could have made him breakfast."

"Not necessary. I'm feeling perfectly fine. Go help yourself. Syrup's in the fridge."

Eliza went to the cupboard and grabbed a plate. She then proceeded to stack the pancakes high.

"You'll have to microwave them for a minute or two," Vera advised.

Eliza listened. Once the ding sounded on the microwave she took them out and smeared them with butter and real maple syrup and dug right in, hungry as a horse who hadn't been fed for a week.

"I have lots of cleaning to do today." Eliza tried to carry on a conversation, but Vera kept getting lost in her own little world. Finally, she responded.

"Jason said the three of you are going to dinner and the movies tonight."

"MIRACLE ON 34TH STREET is playing. The newer, color version"

"Jason said it was a date and that you were going to help him play Santa Claus next week."

"I'm kind of looking forward to picking out presents for Angel. I can't believe Christmas is only two weeks away."

"What's your Christmas wish, Eliza?" Vera set her coffee cup on the table and traced the rim with her now not so frail fingers.

Eliza held her breath. Well, she certainly couldn't tell her the truth. That she wanted Jason and Angel and to see her parents again. So, she came up with the best answer she could give. "I'm wishing for good health next year so that I can be a good care giver."

"That's an unusual wish," Vera said sounding suspicious.

"It's true though," Eliza responded as she crossed her fingers beneath the table. She quickly gobbled up the rest of her pancakes and placed her plate and fork in the dishwasher. "Well, I'm off to clean. Would you like to go to your room?"

"No," Vera said reaching for the paper. "I'm going to sit right here and do the crossword puzzle to pass the time, "By the way, Jason said he had an important conversation planned for you this afternoon."

Eliza lit up. "Yes, and to answer your question, I have only an inkling what he wants to talk to me about."

"He should just propose to you and get it over with," a grumpy Vera added.

"I'll be cleaning the bathroom if you need me."

The morning flew by. Eliza managed to tackle the whole first and second floor, and Angel helped her clean her own room. Otherwise, the little girl stayed busy with her activity books or visiting with her grandmother. Just as she put away the vacuum cleaner, Jason entered the house. Eliza quickly scrambled into her room. She pulled out a pair of Levis, blue and white checked bikini panties with a matching blue bra and an oversized cable knit sweater and headed for the shower. She didn't want to let Jason see her all grimy and sweaty. At exactly three o'clock, Eliza knocked on his door.

"Come in," Jason invited. He had waited all morning for this moment. He wanted to talk to her about her idea, but he also wanted to talk to her about *tonight*.

Eliza opened the door and found Jason perched on the side of his desk. He looked so utterly masculine in his jeans and work boots and heavy knit sweater. Eliza didn't wait to be told to take a seat.

"How's your day going so far?" a casual question.

"If you call cleaning fun, then I had lots of fun today."

Jason chuckled. "I take it you don't like housework."

Eliza laughed along with him. "Actually, no, I don't mind. It takes my mind off of things."

"I just wanted to talk to you about Vera's place. I've found a partner. He's willing to help me get a diner off the ground. We've already got the money needed to upstart the business. Now, we need to find a cook to replicate Mom's recipes and, of course, an entire staff. We still need a place to either build or renovate, so it probably won't get off the ground until late summer, but we'll be working on it."

"That's wonderful," Eliza beamed, "I'm betting your mother will be so flattered. I have her writing down all her recipes in a notebook for me."

"Good. As for the other reason I wanted to see you... Eliza," he looked solemn, "do you consider tonight a date, even though Angel will be with us?"

He blew Eliza away with *that* question. *How to answer without hurting his feelings?* "Jason, it's a date as in we've scheduled some time together."

Jason stood. "I'm asking you if you'd like to go out with me as a man who is interested in dating you."

Eliza felt his mixed emotions. He wanted her badly, she knew that, but he didn't understand her reluctance.

"Eliza, we get along so well. You're wonderful with my Mom and Angel. I just thought maybe there could be something more between us." There. He'd put himself and his feelings on the line.

Eliza couldn't help but be drawn to him. She stood still. A mistake because Jason pulled her close to him. Before Eliza could protest, his lips met hers. He kissed her in a way that every little girl dreams about. He kissed her the way princes kiss their princesses' in fairy tales. He made her tingle from the bottom of her toes to the tip of her head. With all senses on alert, she *felt* Jason's love for her. It overpowered her, but not enough to make Eliza remember her mission and her reward.

Eliza pulled back. "No, Jason. We can't ever be more than employer and friends."

She felt his anger now. "Is there something wrong with me? Is there another man in your life?" he asked running his fingers restlessly through his hair.

"No. There's nothing wrong with you. Any woman would count herself lucky to have someone like you in their life, and you might as well know, I have a date next week with the father of one of Angel's friends."

"Oh," is all Jason could muster. Her admission took the wind right out of his sails, "I'm sorry, I thought you weren't seeing anyone."

"I wasn't when you asked, Jason. I am now," she didn't add the fact that Bill Wiggins didn't interest her in the least and that she never intended to *really* date him. Putting Bill out there like that might encourage Jason to start looking elsewhere. She decided to broach the subject, "Jason, I think you're ready to move on... you're healing. Time has a way of doing that to people."

"Eliza, I'm not even interested in looking at another woman if that's what you're suggesting." He walked around his desk and sat down in the large swivel chair with the high back. "Let's talk about Vera's place. How do you envision it?"

"I see an old-fashioned diner like from the 50s with the staff dressed in that theme. I see meatloaf and beef stroganoff and chicken and peppers and shepherd's pie and cheesecake all on the menu."

"Kind of along the lines of what I think except for the theme part. I think it's a good idea. Hell, look at how Disney does with all of their themed restaurants and hotels. Would you be willing to oversee the décor and costumes? You'd be well paid for it, I might add."

"I think it would be fun."

"I take it that's a yes?"

"Yes," Eliza got up. She felt Jason's sadness, and she just couldn't stay in the room with him a minute longer if that's how he had to feel, "I have to get back to Vera. What time will we be leaving tonight?"

"Five, if that's okay with your schedule."

"I'll meet you in the living room," Eliza said walking out the door. Once back on the first floor, she let the tears flow. The last time she'd cried like this...was when she'd lost Robby. Oh, she knew he went on to a better place, or would be reincarnated and have another life. His soul would live on, but Eliza missed him anyway. His smile. His laughter. His easy going manner, and his strength.

Eliza would do as she told Jason. She'd continue on as a caretaker and would help him with Vera's Place. She wiped her eyes, straightened her sweater and entered the kitchen. Vera sat engrossed in a crossword puzzle.

"Hey," Eliza said softly, "Ever love something and not be able to have it?"

Vera stopped writing and looked up. She noted the tear-stained eyes. "I take it you and Jason had a talk."

"Yeah."

"What did he talk about?" Vera treaded carefully.

"He wanted to know if I'd be interested in dating him."

"And you said no even though you see a life with him."

"Exactly. Vera, I can't explain why, but I do have a very good reason for turning Jason down. I just didn't know how much it would hurt."

"I imagine he's hurting just the same," Vera sighed, "I don't pretend to understand you, Eliza, but if you feel you can't date my son, then so be it. You'll both have to come to terms with your decision, but if you ask me, you should give him a chance. One planned date with another man isn't enough of a good reason for turning down a date with a man you apparently care for very much."

"That's not the reason why, Vera. You'll know one day, when you pass to the other side. Until then help me be strong and resist your son."

"No can do. I feel it right here," Vera thumped her heart, "You two belong together. If I do anything, it's going to be to encourage my son."

Eliza didn't like the direction the conversation headed so, as usual, she changed the subject. "Jason also wanted to talk to me about that idea I gave him. I think it would be so wonderful to have an old fashioned diner serving your recipes. He even liked the name Vera's Place."

Vera's eyebrows rose in surprise. "Why that's quite…that's…what does Jason say about finances?"

"He's found a partner. Now all he needs to do is find a chef who can replicate your recipes, a staff and a location to either build it or buy it. It's going to be a 50s theme. You know, the waitresses in poodle skirts and bobby socks. That kind of thing. I was even thinking there could be a drive-in for malted milk shakes and burgers and fries, stuff like that. Not a McDonald's kind of drive-in, but the kind you see in movies where the girls come out to the cars."

"I remember those days," Vera chuckled, "Henry and I used to always go to Stewarts with the gang. We'd all pile in the car and go for shakes and burgers, just like you said."

"So you think it's a good idea?"

"I think it sounds exciting. I'm flattered, too."

Eliza laughed. "I told Jason you would be."

"Am I that vein that you knew that?"

"No. However, you are very predictable."

"You, however are not," Vera threw down the paper, "Please give this some thought. Tonight, when you're out with my son and Grandbaby, ask yourself how it feels. Does it feel right? If it does, maybe you should fight whatever it is you're struggling with. I don't pretend to know what could possibly stop a young thing like you from having a relationship with a man who would give you more than his heart, but I do know love when I see it. I see it in both your eyes every time you look at each other."

"Am I that transparent?" now the tables turned.

"Yes and no. Any woman who could come into our lives and care for us the way you do… it's more than just an employer-employee relationship. If you love him, take a chance on it. I have a feeling what's stopping you is fear. You're afraid of it not working out and losing a job you like."

"It's not quite that. You are right though, fear is a part of it," *fear of never seeing my parents again.*

"At least try what I said about tonight. Take it from an old woman who knows," Vera reached over and patted Eliza's hand, "Why don't you take a nap. You look like you can use it. You got up awfully early."

Eliza rose, "I think I will. Vera?…thanks for everything."

"It's my pleasure Child. Now scoot. You only have a few hours before you have to get ready."

At exactly five o'clock, Eliza met Jason and Angel in the living room. Angel had her white furry coat and matching hat. Jason stood at attention looking breathtaking in a brown leather bomber jacket and a pair of jeans. As for Eliza, she had chosen a pair of black sweater pants and a long over-sized sweater in a swirl of colors.

"Let's go eat," Jason said. Vera sat on the couch closely monitoring Jason and Eliza.

"Just hand me that remote over there. I plan on watching a little T.V. before I head upstairs."

"Mom, maybe you should just lay on the couch until we get back. I don't want to come home and find you on the floor again."

Vera nodded her agreement. "If I get tired, I have my afghan and couch. Besides, I'll want to hear all about your evening," she looked right at Eliza.

The three of them bade Vera goodbye. Once in the car, Angel spoke up.

"Daddy, while we're at the mall can I get my picture taken with Santa Claus?"

Eliza and Jason exchanged looks. This scene became more family-oriented by the moment.

"Sure, Pumpkin. What do you feel like eating?"

"Pizza," Angel said enthusiastically.

Jason looked over at Eliza in the passenger's side of the car, "and how about you?"

"I think pizza sounds perfect," she smiled back at Angel.

"Pizza it is," Jason said.

Minutes later, Jason pulled into the parking garage. Eliza hopped out of the car and helped Angel unbuckle her seat belt. Jason came around the side and reached for his daughter's hand.

"Wait until you see the Christmas shopping crowd. It's overwhelming," Eliza said to Jason.

"Let's hope there's not too long a line at the pizza place. Movie starts at seven."

"We should be there in plenty of time," Eliza assured him.

Little did Eliza know what a picture the three of them made walking through the mall. People who passed them smiled at the small family that looked like it could grace the cover of a magazine.

They found a seat in the food court, and Jason went for the tray of pizza. Once he came back with that, he returned to the stand for their sodas.

They made small talk over dinner. Jason purposely avoided acting too intimate with Eliza. He tried with all his might to see her as only a nanny, but it did nothing to stop the feelings he had as he watched her eat.

Angel started telling jokes, and the three of them laughed.

"Well, it's time we head on over to the movie theater," Jason announced.

Eliza cleaned up the table and placed the tray on top of the garbage can where others were stacked. Angel grabbed Eliza's hand and her father's. Together, they made their way to the movie theater.

Jason paid for the tickets, and soon the trio located seats in the back of the theater. Angel sat safely between Jason and Eliza. It made Eliza grateful because all she could think about was how it would feel to have Jason's arm around her.

"Popcorn, Daddy. Can I please have some?" Angel batted her big blue eyes and her father scooted off to the snack stand. Once alone, Eliza reminded Angel that they hadn't had time to visit with Santa Claus.

"Maybe Daddy will let me go after the movie. After all, it's not a school night. I can stay up late."

Eliza put her arm around Angel and squeezed her gently, "I'm sure he will. We'll just have to remind him."

Jason returned with an extra large soda and big bucket of popcorn. The movie started.

Eliza leaned over Angel and whispered, "Angel didn't get to see Santa Claus. Do you think we can get her picture taken after the movie?"

Jason looked at his daughter. He'd purposely dressed her in her good hat and coat for the picture. "Sure, I don't see what harm there is in her staying up a little bit later."

"That's exactly what she said," Eliza went back to watching the movie. Angel held the bucket of popcorn between her legs so the three of them could share. At one point during the movie, Eliza dipped her hand in the bucket only to bump hands with Jason.

She looked up at him. He just stared at her. Her heart thumped. He made her feel things she'd never felt before. He didn't move his hand. Instead, he grasped Eliza's hand. For the life of her, she couldn't pull away.

"I think you should reconsider my offer," he said in an even tone.

"Jason…"

"Promise me you'll at least think about it?"

Eliza slowly nodded, "Okay," she gently extracted her hand from the bucket. She definitely hadn't expected Jason to put his arm around Angel and her. For now, she'd enjoy the peace it brought her in feeling Jason's deep devotion to her and his little girl.

"I loved that movie, Daddy," Angel said as she skipped through the mall, "Look! There's Santa!" she let go of Jason and Angel's hands and ran ahead of them to get in line. When the time came for her to go on Santa's lap, she eagerly hopped up.

"What do you want for Christmas little girl?"

"My name's Angel, and the only thing I want Santa is for my Daddy to marry Eliza."

"Well now, that's a tall order. Usually, I just cover toys and clothes."

"That's okay if you can't give me them. Just as long as Eliza becomes my Mommy."

Santa knew this could be a tough spot to be in. "We'll have to see. Is that your Daddy and Eliza," he asked pointing to the handsome couple. Angel nodded an affirmative, "Well, smile for the camera," a flash went off. Angel almost disembarked from Santa's lap, but the girl taking the picture hustled Jason and Eliza to Santa's chair. She put one on either side with Angel still on Santa's lap. Before Eliza could protest, the girl already had taken the picture, "Say Santa Claus," she said as she snapped a second shot.

Angel thanked Santa and walked ahead of Jason and Eliza. Eliza felt Jason's hand on the small of her back like a lightening rod.

Possessive could describe the action. He ordered both pictures from the girl and paid for them. She told them they'd be ready on Monday.

"That'll work out. I'll be here with Angel, Christmas shopping."

He just nodded and grabbed his daughter's hand. "Stay close, Angel. I don't want you getting lost in the crowd."

The ride home seemed too quiet. Jason reached for Eliza's hand. She didn't bother to put up a fight. He squeezed it, "Not so bad, is it?" he asked sounding unsure of himself.

Eliza looked straight ahead. "No, not at all."

"Good," Jason released her hand and turned up the radio which played a Christmas song. Eliza watched as they passed house after house decked out in all colors of lights. Finally, to Eliza's relief, they pulled into Jason's driveway.

When they opened the door, the smell of something baking assailed their senses. Jason walked into the living room, finding his mother sound asleep on the couch. The three of them tip-toed through the room into the kitchen. A hot apple pie sat on the counter with a brief note.

Baked this for three hungry movie goers. Love, Mom

"Well, she can't be asleep too long," Eliza noted, "The pie is still warm."

"How about a scoop of vanilla ice cream on your pie?" Jason looked from Angel to Eliza and back to Angel again.

"Goody! I get to stay up late!"

"Pie, and then it's to bed, young lady," Jason said in his most authoritative voice.

Eliza cut the pie while Jason grabbed the plates and ice cream. He scooped, and Eliza served.

"We're a good team," Jason smiled and it just about broke Eliza's heart, "I think we'll do okay working together on Vera's Place."

Eliza handed him his plate. "I like working with you, Jason. It's no secret."

"Then, maybe you could like seeing me outside of work."

"Maybe," Eliza weakened by the moment. Glory. She had to call Glory tonight so she could talk some sense into her brain that had left her with nothing but strong feelings of security and love and happiness. She couldn't understand how those could be bad things. So, she said a silent prayer to The Big Guy Upstairs.

My Christmas wish, Chief. Do you think it's possible for me to have everything I need because I do need Jason more than my next breath of air. I need his family. Amen.

After they finished their pie and ice cream, Jason addressed Angel. "Come on, I'll put you to bed," to Eliza, he said, "Do you think you could wait down here for me?"

"Sure," she managed to get out. She knew he wanted to pursue the previous topic of conversation without little ears around to hear it.

Fifteen minutes later, he reentered the kitchen. He found Eliza setting the table for the next day's brunch.

"Church tomorrow," a safe enough topic.

"Your Mom is sound asleep. I don't think we should disturb her."

"I agree. Sit down, Eliza, I want to tell you something about Angel."

This immediately got Eliza's attention, *like he didn't already have it from the moment he walked back into the room.*

He sat across from her in Vera's chair. "Kathleen and I married a long time before Angel came along. We both wanted children, but couldn't have them because of a problem Kathleen had. Angel's adopted. We got her as a newborn. Kathleen and I made sure to be there at the hospital when she came into this world. We tried adopting other children, but nothing ever came through for us. Then Kathleen got sick and all that came to a halt. That's why Angel doesn't have any brothers and sisters."

"You're young. You might meet someone someday and have more children."

"I've met her, Eliza. You are everything I've ever wanted in a woman. Don't get me wrong. I loved Kathleen with my heart, but I love you with my soul, and there's quite a difference and quite a surprise to me. I didn't know life after Kathleen existed. From the moment we first met, something just clicked for me. It's like I've known you forever. I know you're my employee, but lots of people who work together date. Please consider a relationship with me beyond that of your boss."

Eliza stayed quiet. She wanted to say yes! Yes! I'll be yours. It clicked for me, too! Instead she simply said, "I'll consider the possibility."

"Can I talk you out of a date next week?"

Eliza lowered her eyes so that her long lashes brushed against her skin. "I'm not really interested in him. Actually, I'm only going because Angel wants a play date with her friend."

"Good," Jason stood and walked around the table. He held out his hand, "Can I have this dance?"

"What?" Eliza asked not understanding.

"Trust me," it was a simple command free of demand.

Eliza put her smaller hand in his much larger one. He led her into the room with the tree. The lights twinkled in the otherwise dark room, and Eliza noticed Vera still sound asleep on the couch, the cream colored afghan covering her from shoulders to feet.

Jason went over to the CD player and put on The Pretender's version of "Have Yourself a Merry Little Christmas." Eliza had to strain her ears to hear the words. It didn't matter to Jason. He pulled her into his arms and began a slow dance. It seemed like time stood still while in his arms. Little did Eliza know, but a very happy old woman watched as her son danced with her beautiful angel.

CHAPTER SEVENTEEN

Even though she could barely hear the music, Eliza felt the warmth of Jason's body all around her. She felt his feelings of contentment and commitment. She closed her eyes and just let herself pretend for a minute that she was a real woman, not an angel. A woman who was free to love a man as strong and caring as Jason. She leaned into him, and felt Jason's chin on the top of her head. The song ended, but neither of them stopped moving. Jason kissed the top of her head.

"Hey," he whispered, "I think it's time for bed," Jason didn't want to push too much, too soon.

Eliza pulled away and looked into his eyes. "Thank you for a wonderful evening. I guess we should go to bed. We have to get up early for mass."

"I could stay here like this all night long, Eliza."

"Me too."

"Come on, I'll walk you to your room," Jason put his arm around Eliza and guided her out of the living room and up the stairs to her bedroom. At the door, he cupped her chin in his hands. "Goodnight," he gently kissed her on the lips. A quiet kiss. A simple kiss. One that promised to take things slowly. Jason withdrew and made his way back to the first floor. There would be no tears tonight. Only dreams of what might be with a beautiful blonde woman one floor above him.

Eliza grabbed the first nightgown she saw and slipped it on. She had never experienced anything like what she had just shared with Jason. Their relationship had taken a step in another direction. The romantically involved direction.

Eliza kneeled beside her bed. "Dear God, I know I never really call you that, but this is too serious an issue for me to be cute and refer to you as The Big Guy Upstairs. I know now I love Jason with all my heart. Angel is like a daughter to me, and Vera the mother I never really got to know. Please give me the strength to make the right decision. I now know I have one to make. If I choose Jason, I forfeit all chances of ever seeing my parents again, though I'll never understand why. If I choose my parents, I lose Jason and his family. As I'm speaking out loud, I'm beginning to understand what you want of me. Your instructions were to not get romantically involved with him. So, I've made my decision that quickly thanks to the feelings you are transmitting to me. I will follow your instructions and only hope you give me the strength I'm going to need to follow through. Amen."

A tear slid down Eliza's cheek. She would never know what it would feel like to be wholly loved by Jason, but at least she had come to a decision. Tomorrow, she would tell Jason there could be no *them*. She'd also tell him she'd stay only until he married again.

Morning came too soon. Eliza dressed in her Sunday best as she liked to call it, and made her way across the hall to Vera's room. She tapped lightly on the door.

"Come in," a voice responded. A cheerful voice.

Eliza opened the door. "I didn't know if you'd be here or still downstairs asleep on the couch."

"No, dear. I woke up and took my time coming up the stairs. I'm thinking things are looking up."

"Yes, but I suggest you still follow doctors orders and take it easy."

"Oh, I'm not talking about my health. I'm talking about life in general. Wouldn't you agree?"

"Oh Vera," she gave her a quick hug, "It's just good to see everyone doing so well. No more nightmares for Angel. Cancer in remission for you and a new project for Jason. I'd say life is looking good."

"What about for you?" Vera smiled a knowing smile. One that said I know something you don't think I know about you and my son.

"You look like the cat that swallowed the proverbial canary. But for me, it's watching the transformation take place. It makes me feel good to know that I'm part of it all."

"We'd better skedaddle before the troops wake up. I'm making crepes this morning. You'll have to pay attention because you're going to be making them for Christmas Day brunch."

"You think I'll catch on that quickly?"

"Oh, they're easy to make, and I'll be right by your side supervising."

"Good because I'd hate to ruin Christmas brunch."

Vera shooed her out the door. Once in the environment she thrived in, Vera stirred up a mixture and showed Eliza exactly what to put in it and how to fry it so that it became a smooth as a pancake crepe.

"Would you get the strawberries and whipped cream out of the fridge, dear?"

Eliza did as asked. That's when she realized it. She always did as asked whether it be Vera or Glory or Jason. Why then shouldn't she do what God asked? That just confirmed it. After church she'd have a talk with Jason. She handed Vera the strawberries and whipped cream and watched her fill and roll the crepes and arrange everything so artfully on a large Lenox platter.

"Hopefully, mine will be as good as yours," a wistful Eliza said out loud without thinking.

"I'm sure they will. So far you've proven yourself as good a cook as Mom," Jason had walked into the room. He had his arm around his mother.

Caught in the act.

Vera didn't miss a beat, "I thought I'd show her how to make them because they can be tricky."

Angel bounced into the room. "Look! Look!" she said holding out her hand. In it she held a small tooth.

"Guess the tooth fairy is going to be making a trip to our house tonight," Jason said as he picked up the tooth, "Let's put it in the tooth fairy bag."

Angel followed her father into the pantry, Rufus, as usual, at her heels.

"There. Now, run upstairs and put it under your pillow so you won't forget."

"Oh, Daddy, I won't forget something *this* important!" Angel made a mad dash for the steps. "Come on, Rufus," the dog needed no prodding.

After a delicious breakfast, the family of four headed out for the church down the street. It never ceased to amaze Eliza how beautiful everything seemed despite its small size. The light filtered through the stained glass windows making everything seem ethereal. An hour later, the group walked through the front door of the modern Victorian Eliza had come to love.

"Jason, could I talk to you in private?" Eliza had pulled him aside, but Vera didn't miss a word.

"We can talk in my office. Is that all right?"

"I'll be right up after I change."

Eliza made it to her room in record time. She quickly changed into a pair of jeans and a pretty lavender and white sweater. She dug in her purse for her cell phone and called Glory.

"I'm doing the right thing, Glory. I just wanted you to know I almost strayed last night. But I realized I had to do what God asked. I just wanted you to know that."

"Eliza, I know it hasn't been easy for you, and you've been confused. Actually, so have I. I've never run into a situation quite like this one and don't understand why God is asking of you what he's asking. It's the right decision though, to follow God's will."

Eliza swallowed the lump in her throat. She felt the unshed tears burning her eyes. "I know. I guess I wanted to hear you say that.

Goodbye, Glory. I've got something important to take care of," she gently closed her cell phone and put it back in her purse. She smoothed her sweater and made her way up the long staircase that led to Jason's office. He stood with the door open and staring out the window.

"Hi," Eliza said as she entered the room. It smelled of Jason's aftershave.

He turned at the sound of her voice and smiled, "I'm glad you wanted to see me alone," he walked over to her and put his hands on her shoulders, "I had a good time last night."

"So did I, Jason. That's what I want to talk about."

He waited.

"I care for you and your family very much, but last night I have to call a mistake. We can't get romantically involved. I'm sorry. I didn't mean to lead you on. I just have to let you know that I'm not going to change my mind, and I hope that you'll respect my wishes."

Jason looked confused and then hurt. "I thought we were going to try…take things slow…"

"No. I have to tell you this. I will stay and work for you until you get married again. That is if you still want me here."

Jason looked down at his feet; then back at Eliza. "I do want you to stay. That just might mean staying until the day I die," he walked out the door without looking back.

Eliza let the tears flow. Now, she had an assignment to complete.

Eliza stood in her spot outside the school. She knew Angel couldn't wait to go to the dollar store and shop for Christmas presents. The minute she spotted Angel she waved. Angel came running.

"Did you bring my money?" a breathless Angel asked.

"I certainly did. You can buy lots of presents."

Bill Wiggins sauntered over to Eliza. "Hey, when would you like to have dinner?"

"I think a play date for Wednesday after school would be great," Eliza put emphasis on play date.

Bill pressed on. "You'll love my spaghetti. I make my own sauce, and it's my grandmother's secret recipe."

"I'm sure we'll love it. Perhaps I can follow you to your house Wednesday?"

"Looking forward to it," Bill's daughter made her way down the pathway to her father, "See you tomorrow, Eliza," Bill waved off, and Eliza sighed. How to gently put Bill in his place? She got a strong feeling that he didn't accept *no* very easily. He seemed a strong-willed man just like someone else she knew. *Stay until he dies. Now that would make a very sad story. Being with the man she loves all of his life without ever getting to really be anything to him but an employee.*

"Let's get going, Shortcake. We've got some Christmas shopping to do," she decided shopping with was Angel the exact thing she needed to take her mind off one very good-looking man with a heart she wanted to own.

Eliza drove to the quaint downtown area. She parked on a side street lined with gingerbread houses. Snow topped the pitched roofs and white picket fences lined the walks. She grabbed Angel's hand and led her around the block to the rather unique dollar store. Outside, it looked like every other house on the street. Inside, it looked like any modern day dollar store. Shelves and shelves of merchandise packed the rather small house. It looked like, at a glance, there would be something for everyone.

"Ooooh! Look at this, Eliza! I think Daddy would love it, don't you?"

Angel picked up the man-sized coffee mug with a picture of a snowman on it.

"I think we'd better get a cart," Eliza said as she made her way over to the area where the carts were kept. She returned and told Angel to put her purchase in the basket. They didn't even get halfway down the first aisle when Angel spotted another gift. She picked up a picture frame with a ceramic fairy on it. "She's beautiful. Like you," Angel deposited the frame into the basket next to the mug, "I think grandma will like that. I'll put the picture of me, Daddy and you and Santa Claus in it."

"Oops! I forgot we have to stop by the mall for it. We'll do that on the way home."

By the time they came to the last aisle, Angel had spent her twenty dollars. She even managed to find a dog bone and squeaky toy for Rufus. They waited patiently in the long check-out line. When the girl at the register started ringing up Angel's purchases she said, "You and your Mommy have done quite a bit of shopping today."

"Oh, she's not my Mommy–yet."

The girl just smiled at Eliza. "You look so much alike."

"Thank you. I'll take that as a compliment," Eliza replied. She touched Angel on the cheek. "We're just doing her Christmas shopping."

"I think these are fine presents. Who are they for?" she addressed Angel.

"My Daddy and grandma. Oh, and my doggie, Rufus."

"Rufus, huh? My dog's name is Lou."

She had Angel's interest. "What kind of dog is he?"

"He's a beagle."

"Like Snoopy?" Angel asked.

"No, he's not all white. He's mostly brown and black with a little bit of white."

The chatty cashier gently wrapped the breakables in heavy paper and packed two bags full of gifts.

"Do you need wrapping paper and bows?" the girl questioned Eliza.

"Actually, we do."

"Here," she said reaching over the counter. "These rolls are all two for a dollar. Pick out which ones you like."

"I don't have enough money," a dejected Angel said.

"I'll buy it, honey," to the girl, she directed, "and we'll take a bag of bows and tags."

Soon, Eliza and Angel packed everything into the car. Once inside, Eliza blasted the heater. "I'll never get used to this bitter cold," she said to a very happy little girl.

"Are we going to the mall now?" Angel asked.

"You bet. It shouldn't take us too long."

It did take long. The line to pick up the photos wrapped around the enclosed area where a Santa-clad man sat with two children on his lap. "I hope your Dad doesn't mind pizza tonight. I'm not going to have much time to make dinner."

"Yum! Pizza! Can we get Gold Crown's?"

Eliza nodded an affirmative. One half hour later, Eliza paid for the pictures. She didn't take them out of the bag until they got in her car. When she did take them out, she just stared at the happy family looking back at her. Angel smiled brightly seated on Santa's lap, and Jason and Eliza took up either side. She looked at Jason. He seemed so... so... happy. So did she. "When we get home, we'll put everything in my room. After dinner, we'll wrap the gifts and put the picture in the frame."

Nothing could have elated Angel more. Eliza punched information on her cell phone and got the pizza place's phone number. She dialed them and ordered two trays of pizza, one with pepperoni.

"Daddy loves pepperoni. I like it plain though. So does grandma," Angel informed a quiet Eliza.

"I'm with your Dad. I just love pepperoni on my pizza," They picked up the pizza and headed home. Once inside, Eliza took their coats and hung them up in the closet. She motioned for Angel to follow her up the stairs. They came to her room and Eliza noticed Vera's door closed. Lately, she'd been leaving it open in the daytime because she spent most of her time downstairs. Just as she opened her door, the door across the hallway opened. Jason stood there, and he had a worried look on his face.

"Am I glad to see you," he said to Eliza, "It's Mom. When I came downstairs to grab something to eat, I found her on the floor again. I carried her up here, and she's been sound asleep ever since."

"Maybe she just wore herself out," Eliza soothed.

"I don't think so. Not this time," it seemed reality finally hit Jason. He claimed Vera not as coherent as she should be.

"Let me stash Angel's presents in my closet, and I'll be right over."

Less than a minute later, Eliza sat down on Vera's bed. She took the woman's older hand in her younger one. Gently she called, "Vera, can you hear me?"

Nothing. Just the irregular breathing that Eliza didn't like. Something definitely was not right. She gently shook Vera, but she still didn't wake up. She turned to Jason. "I think we should let her sleep for awhile. Why don't we go eat the pizza I brought home, and then try again."

Jason nodded as he stared as his mother. She looked better than she had weeks ago, but if honest with himself, she still had a pale complexion and a frail look about her. "Okay," he swallowed the lump in his throat.

Angel didn't say anything as she ate. Eliza tuned into her feelings. Angel *felt* scared. She didn't blame her because, quite honestly, it frightened her too. Jason was another story. His usual voracious appetite seemed to have diminished. He ate one piece of pizza.

"Angel, did you put food in Rufus's dish?"

"I forgot, Daddy. I'll do it now," Angel hurried over to the container containing the dry dog food and put two scoops in Rufus's dish. She came back and reached for another piece of pizza. "Maybe we should save some for grandma. She might wake up hungry."

Eliza patted Angel's hand, "I think that's a good idea, and you may be right. She might wake up hungry as a bear in spring."

No one ate very much, so Eliza wrapped the pizza in foil and put it in the fridge. The three of them made their way back up the stairs. Vera sat up in bed awake now, and it relieved Eliza. Until she got close enough to see that Vera talked nonstop in a whispered hush.

"Mom?" Jason sat alongside her on the bed.

"Oh Henry, I can't wait to see you again. I'm coming. It's my time now. I'll miss Jason and Angel and Eliza."

Vera just stared off into space and continued a conversation with her deceased husband. No matter how hard Jason tried to get her attention, she continued talking with what Eliza thought to be a vision. She knew it not unusual for a person to talk with the *other side* when passing away.

"I'm scared, Henry. You'll be there won't you? I'm coming now," Vera's eyes closed.

Jason turned to Eliza, "Maybe we should just let her rest some more."

Eliza stood behind him, hands on his broad shoulders. "I think I'd better check her pulse."

Jason just nodded his head. Angel stood near the door just watching the scene unfold.

Eliza lifted Vera's limp wrist, "I can't find one, Jason," she put her ear on Vera's chest, "I don't hear a heartbeat. I'm sorry. I think she's gone. We'd better call 911."

CHAPTER EIGHTEEN

It took what seemed to Eliza like an eternity for the ambulance to arrive. The paramedics checked Vera over. The one younger man with the pony tail looked at Jason.

"She's dead. I'm sorry."

"Are you sure?" Jason didn't want to believe it.

The man just simply replied, " Yes."

"Can I have a few minutes alone with her?" Jason asked, his voice unsteady.

The two men left the room.

"I'll go, too. I'm right across the hall if you need me," Eliza hugged Jason.

"Don't go. I don't want to be alone right now."

"What about Angel?" Eliza asked feeling the little girl's sorrow full throttle. He nodded. "You're right. Would you mind taking Angel to her room and talking to her about what she's witnessed?"

"Take your time, and don't worry about Angel. I'll help her understand."

Eliza quietly guided Angel out the door and down the hallway. Once inside her room, Eliza closed the door. Angel laid down on her bed, her face buried in a pillow. Eliza could hear the quiet sobbing and watched as her little body shook. She sat down on the bed. This is what she had to do—as half the purpose for being with the Abbotts in the first place. She stroked Angel's hair.

"Sweetheart, you're grandma is with God now, and your Grandpa and Mommy."

"But, she didn't even say goodbye," Angel hiccupped.

"No, she didn't. That wasn't *her* choice, but she did tell you she loved you every day. Right now, she's looking down on you and praying you have a long and happy life."

"I can't even give her her Christmas presents now," her voice sounded muffled, but Eliza understood. She understood too much what it was like to feel the loss of someone you loved. They didn't even have to die, her relationship with Jason a point in case.

"Angel, I'll be right back."

Angel sat up and rubbed her eyes. "Don't go away, Eliza."

"Honey, I'm just going down the hall to my room. I have something for you from your Grandma."

Eliza quickly went into her room and opened her top dresser drawer. She took out a tiny paper cup wrapped in nylon netting and had a tiny note attached with a pink ribbon. She took a deep breath and prayed the only way she knew how. "Give me strength and guidance, Lord," with that, she went back to a hurting little girl.

She sat back down on the bed. Angel hadn't moved, tears still rolled down her cheeks.

"Your grandmother made this for you last week. She asked me to give this to you when she died," Eliza handed Angel the empty cup, "Do you want me to read the note that's on it?"

Angel nodded.

"This is a very special gift that you can never see. The reason it's so special is it's just for you, from me. Whenever you are lonely, or even feeling blue, you only have to hold this gift and know I think of you. You never can unwrap it, please leave the ribbon tied. Just hold it close to your heart, it's filled with love inside."

Angel sniffled. Eliza opened her arms, and Angel crawled into them. They sat like that, just hugging, Eliza rocking back and forth, for more than an hour. Eliza didn't have time to think about how much she'd miss Vera because her worries now included how father and daughter coped with the situation. When Angel fell asleep, Eliza tucked her in under the covers. She turned off the light and went in search of Jason. She found him in the living room looking at the tree much like the first night she saw him. She touched his shoulder.

"Hey, you all right?"

Jason swallowed. He didn't want to break down in front of Eliza. So far, he'd been able to keep the tears from coming. He didn't look at her. He simply said, "I've had time to prepare for this. Everything is already taken care of."

"I know. You're Mom told me you prepared everything together. Here. I have something for you from her. It's your Christmas present."

Jason looked at Eliza. She felt his overwhelming sadness. "I think you should open it now. I think she would have wanted that."

Jason took the wrapped present from Eliza and opened it. Slowly, he read the words in the framed picture.

My dearest son,

I'll always watch out for you from the other side. When you feel the sunshine, think of me and know that I am happy with others I have loved and who have also passed on. One day we'll meet again. Love transcends time and space. I'll always love you as I know you will me. Be happy and live your life to the fullest for each day is a special gift. Pray for me as I will for you. Until we meet again, my son, my greatest gift from God.

Mom

"I'm always thanking you. You're right, I needed this right now," Jason rubbed his hand over his face.

"Jason, I'll be here for you and Angel for as long as you need me, but I'm going to come clean with something."

Jason had a puzzled expression on his face. Somewhere in his heart he hoped she'd changed her mind as to their relationship.

"I can't cook. You're mother had been preparing every meal for me. Actually, she was in the process of teaching me how to cook. It gave her a sense of purpose. I'm just telling you this because we're going to have order out a lot. I'll try to follow her recipes. She gave me the finished notebook yesterday. You'll have it for Vera's Place."

"It's okay if you can't cook. I would have hired you anyway."

"When's the viewing and funeral?"

"She only wanted one viewing. It'll be Wednesday from four until seven. The funeral will be at ten on Thursday."

"Please let me know if there's anything I can do. Is there a caterer for after the funeral?"

"No. I'm going to call Reno's and set up a brunch."

"Would you like me to handle that?"

"Thanks, but I'll take care of it."

Eliza impulsively bent over and kissed his cheek. "I'll be in my room if you or Angel need me. She's asleep right now."

He just nodded. "Christmas Eve is Saturday. I only wish she could have been here to celebrate with us."

"Me, too. I'm really going to miss her. She's like the mother I never got to really know."

"She liked you. She had hopes of you and me getting together."

"I know that. She didn't make it secret how she felt. Why don't you go rest. You're going to need it to get through the next couple of days. Don't forget we still have to play Santa for Angel. We can go shopping on Friday while she's in school."

"I forgot about that. Can you believe it? My own daughter."

"Don't be so hard on yourself. You're dealing with a lot right now. That's why I'm here... to help you get through this."

Eliza turned and went back to her room. Once safely inside, she cried. She cried for the loss of a good friend. She cried for the loss of Jason as a possible husband. She cried for all the pain she'd felt emanating from both father and daughter. After awhile she stopped long enough to call Glory.

"I know Eliza. You don't even have to tell me. Vera's on the other side. Just know that she's all right, and take care of Jason and Angel."

"I will. Glory?"

"Yes."

"I miss her already. She's just another person I've gotten attached to and won't see again."

"I wouldn't be too sure of that, Eliza. Get some rest. You'll be busy the next couple of days."

"That's exactly what I told Jason," she took a deep breath, "I'm not giving up. I'm going to keep praying that I'll see everyone I've ever loved at least one more time."

"Goodbye, Eliza," Glory hung up first. At least she knew Vera made it to heaven. She knew for certain she made it to her husband. That thought comforted Eliza. Now to get Jason and Angel through the next couple of days.

Tuesday started the influx of food from neighbors, friends and relatives. Eliza graciously greeted everyone at the door or answered the door for delivery people and wrapped much of it in foil or plastic wrap to be stored in the refrigerator for another day or frozen for sometime in the near future. She kept out what she needed to feed Jason and Angel for breakfast, lunch and dinner. She counted her blessings because she received everything from breakfast baskets to homemade lasagna dinners. She had picked out a navy blue dress and black patent leather shoes for Angel for the funeral. She advised Jason to wear his best dark suit. She managed to find time to purchase a simple black dress and pearl necklace and earrings to match for herself. Jason showed Eliza the dress that Vera had picked out months ago for her burial. A soft rose suit, size four. Eliza knew the undertaker would have to tuck it in because Vera had lost so much weight.

Wednesday came too quickly. Before she realized what happened, she stood in line beside Jason and Angel in a funeral home. Jason had insisted she be with them throughout the whole ordeal. Not until Thursday morning as she sat grave side with Jason and Angel did it really hit her. *No more Vera. No more morning chats while her mentor cooked up a delicious breakfast. No more hearing her insist she was perfect for her Son and Grandbaby. No more anything.* It made Eliza wonder when she'd ever be able to go to the other side of heaven. The side where souls stayed for eternity. She knew in her heart just from talking to Vera she'd found her soulmate in Henry, and they now experienced eternity together. What did she do wrong that she couldn't go there? She had questions and no answers. What did Glory mean when she said maybe there would be a reunion of souls? How on earth could she find Jason a new wife? He insisted more than once that she would be with him until the day he died. That is if she meant what she said–that she'd stay until he got married. That pretty much made the other half of her assignment virtually impossible–if he wasn't willing to even consider another woman.

The professionals lowered the coffin into the frozen ground. Angel followed her father's lead and dropped her rose into the hole and turned to leave. Jason grabbed her hand. Eliza and the others gathered around took their cue and started to disperse. They all met at Reno's restaurant for brunch. Jason had made sure there would be enough food for everyone who wanted to attend. Eliza stood in line at the buffet table behind Jason. She had Angel's dish as well as one for herself.

"What would you like, sweetie?" she asked Angel.

"French toast please," Angel said quietly. Eliza felt her sadness, "I bet it won't be as good as grandma's."

"I'm sure it won't."

Jason turned around and looked at Eliza. "Do you really believe in an afterlife?"

"As sure as I'm standing here," she said, "She's with God now and her family and friends. She had a good, long life, Jason. I don't know why we have to say goodbye to those we love, but I think most of us will see our loved ones again one day."

"You help me believe," he turned back to the table and filled his plate with scrambled eggs and bacon. *Well at least he was going to eat,* Eliza thought. She filled her own plate with French toast and syrup. The three of them walked to their table in the corner of the room.

"I didn't want to be front and center today," Jason explained, "I'd prefer to be alone with you and Angel."

"Eat up, Jason. You've got to keep up your strength. Christmas Eve is only two days away."

Angel managed a smile. "Maybe Santa Claus can take my presents and give them to grandma."

"I think that's a great idea. We'll leave them with the milk and cookies," Eliza put her arm around Angel and squeezed, "We'll leave him a letter explaining what happened."

"Okay. I can't wait for Santa, Daddy."

"You've been an exceptionally good girl this year. I'm betting you get lots of presents."

Eliza felt the tension go away, *at least for now.* She had to keep them focused on the positive things in life and how happy they should be during the holidays.

Once back at Jason's house, Eliza breathed a sigh of relief. The quiet felt ominous. Now she started to *feel* a sense of acceptance from both Jason and Angel. They'd certainly had enough time to prepare for Vera's death. Thank God her *feelings* came back. She thought about her parent's death–unexpected and tragic. She'd finally come to terms with the fact she'd never see them again until the day Glory told her she could see them if she completed this assignment. How to get Jason to believe he should move on without her? Maybe in time…If she knew one thing it had to do with her heart and it would always be heavy because she had to give up the only man she'd ever loved. Maybe being with her Mom and Dad would make up for that. *Could that kind of love take the place of romantic type of love?* She wondered.

Jason had gone up to his office to work in order to keep his mind busy with something other than thoughts of his loss. Angel retreated to her room saying she wanted to play with her dolls. It left Eliza free to play her harp. She sat at the oversized instrument and plucked away. She knew, no, she *felt*, how it calmed Jason and Angel even from the distance. They loved when she played for them.

Jason dropped Angel off at school as usual on Friday morning. When he returned, he found Eliza seated on the living room couch, coat and boots on. He didn't have to say anything. She automatically got up and followed him to his car. They communicated sometimes without saying a word–like they'd known each other forever.

It had snowed the night before, only lightly, but enough to make the roads a little bit slick. Jason drove slowly.

"Do you know what she wants for Christmas?" Eliza asked.

"You. As her step Mommy. She gave me her list last week, and that topped it."

Eliza knew she had to be careful here. "What else is on it?"

Jason dropped the subject of her as a stepmother to Angel. He knew her to be a hopeless cause. With his mother around prodding her and encouraging her to look his way, meant hope. "She wants a Disney princess bike. A Barbie computer and surprises."

"Well that's an easy enough order to fill. We can have some fun picking out surprises. Where are we going by the way?"

"The Toy Shop. They have a sale on bikes. I don't know about the computer."

"We'll be able to pick out some really interesting software for her. I know there's one with Clifford and Winnie the Pooh. She loves both of them."

Jason knew taking Eliza along to be a good idea. It just hadn't turned out to be the *date* he had hoped for. "I take it you canceled your play date?"

Eliza's hand flew to her mouth. "With everything going on, I forgot to call Bill. He'll understand though."

"Eliza, you're more than welcome to bring him to my house. It's up to you who you choose to see."

"Does that mean you're ready to move on from me?" she had to be direct with him. She knew his feelings, but she couldn't read his mind.

"I have no problem being single for the rest of my life," Jason pulled into a parking spot. Thank heavens they reached the toy store. It would take Jason's mind off of her, for a while anyway.

Together, they carefully selected dolls and clothes and stuffed animals they thought Angel would immediately fall in love with. They didn't forget Rufus. They bought him a pair of deer antlers. Jason actually smiled when Eliza suggested them. It *felt* good to see him smile. It also *felt* right being by his side picking out his little girl's

Christmas presents. She'd never played Santa before so she made the most of it tossing in odds and ends here and there. She decided if she could only do this once she would do it right–go all out. Jason didn't seem to care about the huge bill Eliza racked up as she pushed the cart through the aisles, stopping every so often to add a treasure to their pile of rapidly growing Christmas presents. Finally, they checked out. Eliza ignored the cashier when she gave the final tally. She didn't want to hear how much of Jason's money she just spent.

Jason laid his hand on her arm and like a lightening rod, she felt the electric jolt.

"I needed you here with me today. I just want to say thank you. I hope you know I don't expect you to recreate my mother's Christmas morning breakfast and dinner."

"Oh," Eliza said with a smile on her lips, "are you afraid I'll kill both of you with my cooking?"

Jason actually laughed out loud. Thank God they could get past the word killed.

"I'm really just giving you a break. I can order from our local bakery and restaurant."

Eliza crossed her hands over her chest. "I WILL give you the breakfast and dinner Vera made me promise to make for you and Angel."

"Give it up man," said the guy with a cart piled high with toys behind them, "she means business. Just eat it and say you like it."

Jason turned to him. "I will like it because she cooks just like my mother," he turned back to Eliza, "Fine. The challenge is on. You do both. If you can't, I'll order out or we'll use some of the stuff in the freezer."

"Hmph," Eliza managed to get out, now more determined than ever to prove that Vera had actually taught her a few things.

CHAPTER NINETEEN

"Well that's quite a haul," Jason said as he wiped his brow. He'd carried everything in and hid it in the two closets closest to the tree room.

"I know how to shop. I may not be the world's best chef, but I do know how to pick out presents," she motioned for Jason to look beneath the tree. He saw a couple of boxes with his name on them, and the *from* said, Eliza. It made him long for her to just admit she felt the same way he did. She didn't act like a woman who didn't care. Everything she did, and everything about her spoke of her love for him and his little girl. If he could have one Christmas wish... *Why even go there?* He had to learn to accept that to have Eliza continue on with him, he had to remain single. He had no problem with that. Yes, he'd like to make love to her. Yes, he'd like to kiss her whenever he felt like it. Not to be able to do so would be painful to say the least, but less painful than the alternative? *No Eliza in his life?* He'd use Vera's Place as a way to get even closer to her. What did his mother say to him just before she died? She'd mumbled something about Eliza being *tested by the Good Lord above*. Whatever that meant, it didn't mean she'd agree to be his wife and Angel's mother.

"I'm sure Angel will have us up early tomorrow morning," Jason said it in a matter of fact tone.

"Do you think I don't want to see it?" Eliza asked. For the first time she felt her temper rise. How could this man she... she... loved even make a statement like that. Early didn't matter to her. Love made it so that she would be there for Angel–and her father.

"I'm sorry. I didn't realize it meant so much to you," Jason baited her.

"Yeah, well it does. That little girl of yours could be my own. I want to see her smile again and laugh. It's bad enough she lost her first mother and then grandmother...but, she doesn't need to lose me."

Eliza turned her back on Jason. He sighed. She did care. She did love them. Time...that's all it meant... a matter of time. For the first time in a long time Jason felt hopeful.

"I'll wake you the minute she's up," Jason said without touching her though everything in him made him want to hold her.

"Good. Because I want to be there for the good times as well," Eliza turned on her heel. Then, she realized what she'd said. Jason didn't miss a beat.

"In sickness and in health 'till death do us part," he firmly walked away from the woman who held his heart in the palm of her hand.

Eliza blinked. Oh, God, what had she said? And why? She decided the best mode of operation or the safest meant going to bed and then waking with Angel Christmas morning.

"Please wake me when Angel gets up," Eliza's anger rang true, but Jason now understood why. She loved them as much as they loved her.

The next morning came early. At 5 a.m. Angel bounded out of her bed, Rufus on her heels. "Santy, Santy Claus has been here," she yelled throughout the halls and down the stairs.

Both Jason and Eliza had to shake themselves awake. Eliza had on her flannel nightgown and slippers when she bumped into Jason in his red plaid robe in the hall.

"I guess Santa comes early," is all Eliza said to Jason not realizing he'd slept in the master bedroom for the first time since she'd known him.

By the time they reached the tree room papers flew everywhere. It felt so good to see such happiness after all the bad they'd seen. Eliza giggled and laughed and clapped whenever Angel showed her a new toy or doll. Jason stayed quiet. The only thing on his mind, no matter how much he loved his daughter, was Eliza. She fit into their life perfectly.

"Time for the Christmas crepes," Eliza announced as Angel opened the last of her presents.

"Yeah! Will they taste like grandma's?" an inquisitive Angel asked.

"I'll try my best," Angel said meaning every word. She had the recipe right there in front of her. She could do it. Yes, she could do it, and she did—to her surprise. She actually made something Vera would have been proud of.

"It's good," Jason said, "Better than good," he continued, "if I didn't know better I'd think my Mom sent you a few messages."

Eliza couldn't help but reach out and touch Jason's hand, "She is because I could never do this by myself."

Jason chose to ignore that and continued a conversation with Angel.

Christmas dinner meant more of the same. Eliza shocked Jason with her culinary skills though followed line by line on the recipe notes Vera had left behind.

At long last, Christmas Day concluded. Angel seemed happy enough...and Rufus...he just didn't know when to stop wagging his tail. As for Jason...he seemed pensive. Eliza wished him a good night.

"Eliza, could you at least think about some of the things I've said before today?"

"Promise," Eliza smiled at him a genuine smile. One that tugged on his heart. She didn't mean to lead him on...only offer him hope.

He leaned in and gave her a kiss meant for fairy princesses. He looked up at her and noticed how wide-eyed she seemed. "We all have our Christmas wishes. That is mine," he walked away.

"What is?" Eliza sputtered.

You'll figure out, maybe some day," Jason headed straight for his room.

Eliza grasped her Mother's hand, "Oh, Mom, I've waited so long," a tear slowly slid down Eliza's cheek.

"I know dear, but everything is going to be all right."

Eliza turned to her Father who in turn gave her a bear hug. "We're happy here," he whispered into her ear.

"We have eternal love...something many souls don't achieve."

"Oh, Mom, God wants me to make a choice. Stay with you and Daddy or go back on earth for a wonderful man I've met and his baby girl."

"It shouldn't be a hard decision, Eliza. Do you love the man and his daughter?"

"Yes, she does," Eliza startled at the voice. She turned to Vera's familiar voice, "and my Boy and little Grandbaby need a good mother and wife. By the way, I'm Vera," She shook Eiza's parent's hands, "Thanks to your daughter, happiness always seemed to be in my house when it could have been different."

"Oh, Vera!" Eliza embraced her, "I've missed you so."

"No, you miss my cooking," Eliza and Vera shared a secret smile.

"Hi, Eliza," Angel walked up to her decked out in her little white dress with her black patent leather shoes. She grabbed Eliza's hand.

"What are you doing here?" Eliza asked clearly puzzled.

"I'm here to make sure you come back with me to be my new Mommy. I met my Mommy, and she said it's okay. You and Daddy are soulmates, and she founded her soulmate, and that one day when I grew up I'd understand."

Eliza woke up. Oh, God. Her dream seemed so real. She needed her parents. She knew now what she should tell Glory. She'd go back to her parents. Her dream left her unsettled.

Angel sat across from Eliza at the breakfast table that now held one empty seat. She looked at Eliza and said, "Your Mommy and Daddy are nice. I'm glad I got to talk to my Mommy again. She'll always be my Mommy."

She took Eliza by surprise, "Honey, what do you know about my parents?"

"That they love you and want you happy. I was there you know," Angel winked.

For the first time Eliza realized her dream couldn't really have been a dream. She met with her parents. "Oh, thank you God wherever you are," she whispered.

Angel didn't miss a beat. "You passed the test, Eliza."

That night, Jason approached Eliza not sure what to say, "What...you and Angel talked about this morning at the breakfast table?"

"Oh, a dream I had."

"Angel said she met your parents, but Eliza they're deceased."

"Oh, I think Angel has an active imagination."

"I think there is something you're not telling me," Jason grabbed Eliza by the hands, "If you ever need to talk to someone about your parents, you know you can always come to me. Eliza, I want you as my wife and Angel's mother. You've avoided me for days and haven't given me your answer.

Eliza looked into Jason's chocolate colored eyes, and she felt the now familiar butterflies in her stomach. *Oh, what would it be like to be held by this strong, caring, gentle man every night? What would it be like to always have Angel in her life? What would it be like to have Jason's babies?*

She knew she had to have him, but first she had to talk to Glory. "Give me a couple of days, Jason. It's just that I'm not prepared for this," *falling in love with you, she said silently.*

"Fine. Take all the time you need because there's no one else for me."

Eliza stood on tip-toe and kissed Jason on the cheek.

"Thank you. Now, there's somewhere I have to go. Can you take care of Angel?"

"Yes, but I want you to think about what I said. I mean talking about your parents. It helped me to talk about Kathleen and Mom."

"I will think about it Jason, more than you'll ever know."

Glory sat on the park bench with a sleeveless dress on despite the cold weather. Eliza had to smile. She remembered how she used to do that before she had to act and dress *human*.

"You rang?" Glory smiled.

"Yes, Glory, I have something heavy weighing on my mind. I believe I've seen my parents and have a choice now to go to them or stay with Jason and Angel."

"Maybe you have seen your parents," the wiser, older angel replied.

"Maybe it is God's way of saying you do have a choice to make and is giving you one more chance to see your Mom and Dad."

"But, why would he do that?"

"So you can make the right choice?"

"Glory, if I stay with Jason and Angel what happens to me?"

"You become human like them–though you'll always have a little angel in you, "Glory smiled softly, "Your *feelings?*"

"And then I'll never see my parents again?"

"Now that is a different story. When your natural time for death comes, you'll be reunited with your family."

"I'll see them again, just not for another sixty-years or so?"

"Since when do you know when you're going to die? It could be a month from now you know."

"Oh, Glory, it's so confusing. I love them, but I love Jason and Angel and so desperately want to be a family."

"I can't tell you what to do, Eliza, but I can give you some advice. Sixty-years in heaven is like a day on earth. Now, I must leave. Whatever you decide, I want you to know you are a wonderful angel and deserve whatever will bring you happiness. I think you passed His test. Assignment completed," Glory turned, walked behind a tree and simply disappeared.

Eliza tied her scarf tighter and put her gloved hands in her pockets. Time to talk to Jason. Honestly. She would tell him the whole truth and see how he took it. Maybe he'd think her crazy.

Eliza pulled up to the house that had been her home for a short time. She wondered how Jason would feel once she told him everything. After all, if he wanted her to be his wife, she wanted him to understand her *feelings*.

She walked up the stairs thinking about what exactly she would say. She didn't even reach the door when it opened. Jason stood there so masculine, so incredibly handsome that she wanted to run into his arms and forget everything except how it *felt* to be with him.

"Hi. Saw you pull up," Jason opened the conversation. He looked concerned, "Are you all right?"

"Oh, me?" Elisa said snapping out of it, "I…uh…need to talk to you."

Jason smiled as he helped her with her coat. She had on a pants suit in his favorite color on her, pink.

"Want to go to the kitchen and have some coffee?"

"Jason, why don't we go into the family room. Where's Angel?"

"She's upstairs playing, why?"

"What I have to say is just between you and me."

"Fine," Jason said. He put his hand on the small of her back and guided her into the room with the glorious over-sized Christmas tree. Even though it was mid-day, the lights still twinkled.

Jason sat first and patted the couch cushion next to his. Eliza obeyed his silent command.

"Jason, I'm not what I seem."

He waited.

"I'm really an angel sent to help you with your mother and to find you a wife and mother for Angel."

"I'll agree. You are an angel, and you did do both of those things. You helped me with my grieving for Mom, and I found Angel a mother. You. I want you as my wife."

"No, no, no, Jason," Eliza got flustered, "I mean, I'm really an angel from heaven. I died with my parents in that car crash. They went to one part of heaven, and I went to angel training school."

"Okay," Jason didn't know what to say. He loved Eliza, and he knew her to be completely sane at all times. He also understood this could be her way of dealing with her grief.

"Jason, if I choose to become your wife, I won't get to see my parents and Vera again until I die a natural earth life."

"And if you don't choose to marry me?"

"I go to heaven to be with my parents for all eternity."

"And then I'll have to die a natural earth life before I can be with you again," he said pensively. Something dinged in his brain. Maybe she really believed what she said.

Apparently, he believed her, Eliza thought. "What about Kathleen? I always thought you'd want to be with her again."

"I thought so until I met you. I think of her now as a first love. Someone preparing me for something even more fulfilling."

A lone tear slipped down Eliza's face, "I do love you."

"Then be my wife, and we'll all be together in the end."

Eliza's heartbeat sped up. Oh how she wanted to say yes.

Angel stepped into the room. "I always knew you wanted to be my Mommy."

Eliza gathered Angel into her arms. "I always knew The Big Guy Upstairs would give me my Christmas wish."

Jason included himself in the hug. His lips met Eliza's. "And I always knew I'd get my holiday kiss."

Angel beamed as her father kissed her new Mother-to-be.

Eliza couldn't help thinking about Christmas wishes and holiday kisses...

Printed in the United States
66285LVS00002B/64

9 781424 146840